Together Apart

Together Apart

by

DIANNE E. GRAY

Houghton Mifflin Company
BOSTON

A poem by Ted Kooser, published in his book *The Blizzard Voices* (1986), was excerpted with the permission of the Bieler Press, Minneapolis, Minnesota.

The text of this book is set in Centaur MT.

Library of Congress Cataloging-in-Publication Data
Gray, Dianne E.
Together apart / by Dianne E. Gray.
p. cm.
Summary: In 1888 in Prairie Hill, Nebraska, a few months after barely surviving a deadly blizzard
that has killed two of her brothers, fourteen-year-old Hannah goes to work at the home of a
wealthy widow with progressive social ideas, where she finds Isaac, who is also trying to make a new
life for himself. Told from alternating points of view of Hannah and Isaac.
ISBN 0-618-18721-9 (hardcover)
[1. Sex role—Fiction. 2. Blizzards—Fiction. 3. Grief—Fiction. 4. Nebraska—History—19th
century—Fiction.] I. Title.
PZ7.G7763 To 2002
[Fic]—dc21
2002000408

Manufactured in the United States of America
QUM 10 9 8 7 6 5 4 3 2

For my husband, Lee,
who was, is, and will always be—my Isaac

Acknowledgments

Many and heartfelt thanks go to the following people: Mary François Rockcastle and the Graduate Liberal Studies Program at Hamline University for their continued encouragement and support; Kirsten Dierking, Kay Korsgaard, Sue Montgomery, and Kathy MacKnight, dear friends and inexhaustible cheerleaders; Amy Flynn for her patience and brilliant editing; my Nebraska family, for always welcoming me home; my daughters, Leanne Knott and Shelley Paulson, who bring joy to my life; and my husband, Lee, who lights and lightens my days with his love.

Visit the author's Web site at *www.prairievoices.com.*

. . . the wind in the hedgerow,

the wind lifting the dust

in the empty schools,

the wind which in the tin fan

of the windmill catches,

turning the wheel to the north—

that wind remembers their names.

—Ted Kooser, from
The Blizzard Voices

PART I

Early May, 1888

Hannah

WE MUST HAVE MADE A SORRY SIGHT, MY BROTHER, SISTER, and me, hurrying along the wooden sidewalk, soaked to the bone. The sky had been a gloomy gray when we'd left Fowler's Emporium on Main Street, and there had been only a misty hint of rain when we'd stopped by Papa's farm wagon to drop off our trades — eggs and butter for a tin of chamomile tea, lamp oil and wicks, and a paper of sewing needles. Halfway to the place I hoped would be my chance at a fresh start, the wind had begun to gust and the rain to pour. I was greatly annoyed, though not surprised. I'd lived all my life on the Nebraska prairie. Lightning-quick changes in the weather were as common as flies around a milk bucket.

We were about to cross a puddle-pocked street when Joey, his jaw chattering, looked up at me and said, "I'm cold."

I scooped him up. "Make believe that you are the captain of a sailing ship and the rain is spray from a warm-water sea."

"A big ship?"

"Yes, a very big ship."

Megan tugged at my skirts. "Are there pretty ladies on the ship, too?"

"Fine ladies in fancy dresses," I answered just as a team and freight wagon sped past, splattering us with filthy water.

"Change that to a steamboat on the muddy Missouri. A steamboat that must make haste. If we're not back at the wagon when Papa's ready to start for home, it will be a month of Sundays before he allows us to come to town with him again." What I didn't say was that it would probably be a month of Sundays before *I* came to town again — late to the wagon or not. Mama could only spare one of us older girls, and more often than not I was the one who drew the shortest straw when it came to deciding who would go. My being in town that day, heading where I was heading, was a wonder in and of itself.

Rows of tidy, wood-framed houses lined either side of the street. Some were watched over by picket fences; some had stone paths that led to sturdy-looking front doors. Most were painted white, and I wondered why this was so. Orange, plum, or apple red would be easier to find in a blinding snow.

Two street crossings farther along, we arrived at the edge of town. The sidewalk angled off to the right, but I saw only the prairie beyond. The wild grasses, fresh up after the long winter and wetted a deep and fragrant green, swept me up in a moment of forgetfulness. My bones felt lighter, my breathing easier, and I left myself standing there, Joey on my hip, Megan at my side, and imagined myself into the prairie, arms spread wide, turning in circles until dizzy with the joy of it. A hint of music, far off in the distance, kept time.

I'd been drawn to the openness of the prairie for as long as I remembered, and, according to Mama, for even longer than that. Of her nine babies, I'd been the most impatient to get myself born, and once born, the hardest for her to keep her eye on. I'd made my first trek into the world of grasses and wildflowers and sky when I was only eleven months old. When Mama found me two frantic hours later, she said I wasn't scared and crying like she'd expected. I looked up at her, grinned, then turned and toddled away. And that had only been the beginning.

The longer my legs grew, the faster and farther away I wandered. I imagined myself the wild, galloping stallion or the red-tailed hawk, soaring circles against the empty sky. The butterfly. The prairie air seemed easier to breathe than the stale and crowded air inside our sod house. There was more room to think out there. More room to let my body move in whatever way it wanted. Mama had tried to put a stop to my wandering — with a spank when I was little and by assigning me extra chores when I got older — but I'd always found a way, always found the time. While my brothers and sisters kept to the road on their way to and from Harmony School, more often than not I chose a prairie path. As the years passed, more and more of the prairie had been plowed into fields, but enough remained to draw me in. Until the blizzard, which reared in my imagination just then, stomped my chest, choked my breath, blinded my eyes with white, swallowed me.

A tug on my hand pulled me back. "Look, Hannah," Megan said. "It's a castle, like the one in the picture book at school."

The blizzard shrank back into hiding. Breath returned. My vision cleared, and I looked in the direction Megan was pointing. "Nearly so," I answered.

Megan let go of my hand then and began to run along the angled sidewalk. She hadn't gone far when she stumbled on an uneven plank and fell. I caught up to her, lowered Joey to the sidewalk, and then bent over Megan. Blood seeped from a small cut on her quivering chin. I lifted my skirt modest inches, thinking to dab at the blood with the hem of my petticoat. The bleached muslin was caked with mud. There was nothing to do save untuck the tail of my white shirtwaist.

As I dabbed, I glanced first at the house and then in the direction we had come. Turning back before some worse calamity befell us seemed the sensible choice, and I might have done just that if not for the promise of the handbill I'd found posted at Fowler's and memorized as if a part in a school play. "Ready?" I asked. Megan nodded and slipped her hand into mine. I took Joey's hand in the other, and we walked on.

Standing alone at the edge of the prairie, the house was built of *red* brick and rose three stories under a many-gabled roof. Stone arches, like curious brows, topped each of the many windows. Painted trim that put me in mind of wooden teeth decorated the spaces beneath the eaves. Attached to a rear corner of the house was a one-story frame building, and attached to this was a smallish barn. It was an arrangement the likes of which I'd never seen, though I thought it quite clever. One could go from house to barn without being tormented by the weather. A brick drive, laid out in a crisscross pattern, entered the property at one point along the dirt street, curved, and then returned to the street at another, like a rust-red rainbow. Trees of varying size and variety dotted the lawn.

I'd meant to make my inquiry at a rear door but chose instead the wide veranda that wrapped the front of the house. Its roof would get us out from under the rain, if only for a little while. We scraped the mud from our shoes as best we could in the grass next to the stone path, then climbed the steps slowly, as if the steps to a church.

It wasn't until I stood before the mirrorlike glass oval in the door that my heart scolded me for my foolishness. My hair looked like a mop just used to wash the floor. My lips were blue, and my sopping shirtwaist clung like another layer of skin. Foolish, indeed. The handbill had asked for a "Clever and Forward-Thinking Young Person." I was only fourteen. I knew next to nothing about town life and even less about the duties an "Apprentice in a Growing Business Concern" might require. Fresh starts being about as hard to find as a four-leaf clover, I wasn't about to leave until I'd at least had a chance to come face to face with mine.

Thinking the brass knocker too bold, I rapped lightly with my knuckles. I waited for what seemed a fitting length of time and rapped again. Still no one answered. I clapped the knocker, thrice and loud enough to wake the dead. Then, just as we turned to leave, Joey said, "I have to go."

"But you've only just arrived."

I spun around. Standing there at the open door was the most peculiar town woman I'd ever seen. Her cinnamon-colored hair was mussed. Her ivory cheeks were smudged with black, as were her hands and the full-length canvas apron she wore. She was youngish, early thirties perhaps, too young to be the lady of so grand a house, the widow of the Judge Harlan Moore of the handbill. Surely the position had been filled. The words I'd planned to say stuck in my throat, causing me to hiccup.

"I'd offer my hand, but you can see that it's stained with printer's ink. My name is Eliza Moore. Eliza if you have come as a friend, the Widow Moore if you have not."

I hiccupped again, then said, "I am Hannah Barnett, and this is my brother, Joey, and sister, Megan."

Joey squeezed my hand. I looked down at him and saw from the pained look on his face that asking him to wait wouldn't do. "I've come to ask about the position. But first we need to go around back and use your necessary house."

Eliza smiled. "There's no need to go around back, especially in this rain. I have a water closet inside."

"Oh, no, we mustn't. Our shoes" — hiccup — "are soiled."

"Remove them, then," she said, scandalously sliding a shoeless foot out from under the hem of her skirt and wiggling it around.

Megan, whose shoes had been passed down through three sisters and were yet two sizes too large, was in her stocking feet quicker than a frightened prairie dog down its hole. Before I could catch up her hand, she had darted through the door. There was nothing to be done save remove mine and Joey's shoes and follow after her.

I found her standing stone still with her mouth agape in front of a larger-than-life portrait that hung in the wide front hall. The portrait was of a handsome, finely dressed woman.

"Is she a queen?" Megan whispered.

"Not quite. Though there was a time when I thought her my fairy godmother. This is my late husband's mother, Madeline Moore. She was the kindest woman I have ever known." Eliza took up Joey's hand then and said, "This way to the water closet."

I followed Eliza down the wood-paneled hall, lifting my skirts so as not to leave a trail of mud on the wine-colored carpets. Megan zigzagged from one side of the hall to the other, peeking into every room. I couldn't blame her. Truth be told, if I hadn't been there to apply for a position, I wouldn't have minded peeking myself.

At the end of the hall, we turned and passed through the kitchen before stopping at the door to the indoor necessary. "Do you know how a water closet works?" Eliza asked Joey.

Joey hid his face in my skirts. Eliza winked at me and said, "Just pull the chain when he's finished. In the meantime I'll gather up some amusements to entertain the children."

I nodded, hiccupped, and then shepherded the little ones inside and closed the door behind us. Joey took one look at the indoor necessary, crossed his arms over his chest, and said, "I don't have to go anymore."

"None of that, young man. You said you had to go, and we've put Mrs. Moore to all the trouble, so you'll go."

"I won't."

"Oh, yes you will, and you'll do it now. Just make believe that you are a king and the indoor necessary is your throne."

"Do I have a crown?"

"The biggest crown ever."

"Me too? Can I be a queen and have a crown too?" Megan asked.

"Yes, of course, but be quick about it."

While the young ones were using the royal throne, I stood at the sink and turned one of the spigots. Water, as if by magic, gushed out and into my hands. Warm water! Warm, then running hot as I gulped handfuls, hoping to drown my hiccups.

———————

Back in the kitchen, Megan and Joey sat together on a pressed-back chair. Open on the table before them was a picture book of fairy tales, the pages of which Megan carefully turned. Milk mustaches outlined their smiles.

I, too, sat at the table, staring at the pattern of leaves in the bottom of a dainty teacup. We would need to be leaving soon, so I knew I mustn't tarry. I returned the teacup to its saucer with a rattle and was about to tell Eliza that I believed myself to be a hard worker when she asked, "Has your mother sent you to inquire after the position?"

"No, ma'am. I've come on my own." I wasn't sure this was the wisest answer, though it was the truthful one.

She smiled. "If offered the position, could your mother spare you?"

"I have one older sister, Hester, who is seventeen, and another sister, Lila, who is a year younger than I am."

"And how old might you be?"

I squared my shoulders. "I will turn fifteen in October."

Eliza's left brow arched, if but a sliver. "Do you attend one of the country schools?" she asked.

"We've been without a teacher since the . . . since January," I stammered.

"Oh, my. Not Harmony School?"

My feet, badly frostbitten in the blizzard, prickled as if I were walking barefoot in a patch of thorny thistle. I lowered my head. "Yes, ma'am."

I could feel Eliza's eyes studying me, and after a bit she said, "I must be honest with you, Hannah. I filled the position earlier today, though I've been thinking that perhaps I might allow for two. Would it be possible for you to return tomorrow morning, prepared to stay on a trial basis through the end of the week?"

The thistle patch turned into a field of ticklish clover, and my eyes shot up. "I could be here by nine, if that's not too late?"

"Nine will be fine. And I've a question I'd like you to think over and answer for me when you return. If suddenly you found yourself quite alone in the world, your only assets a grand house and quickly dwindling funds, what clever, yet tasteful, endeavors might you undertake to support yourself? Turning this fine home into a boarding house or taking in wash are not the class of answers I'm hoping for."

Megan and Joey weren't anxious to quit the fairy tale book until I reminded them about the month of Sundays. We said our goodbyes to Eliza on the veranda, laced our muddy shoes, and then hurried down the steps. The rain had ended, and here and there the sky showed patches of blue. Though we followed the same sidewalks returning as going, the distance to Main Street seemed as if half.

I was greatly relieved when we reached the town square and found that Papa hadn't yet returned to the wagon. Hap and Hazard, Papa's team of Belgian horses, his pride, whinnied in greeting. I lifted Megan and Joey into the back of the wagon and told them to wait there, then dashed across the street, startled the bell above the door to Fowler's Emporium, and strode to the place on the wall where the handbill was tacked. Once it was in my pocket, I turned on my heel, hiccupped, and startled the bell once again on my way out.

We waited another hour for Papa. Megan and Joey bided the time napping, their heads resting in my lap. I bided my time mulling over Eliza's question.

———

"Did you trade for everything on your mother's list?" Papa asked when he climbed onto the seat of the wagon.

"Yes, sir," I answered.

Megan rubbed the sleep from her eyes, and before I

could hush her with a finger to my lips, she said, "Hannah took us to a castle."

Papa seemed not to hear, and I was glad for this. I wanted to wait until after supper, when I had Papa and Mama together, to tell them my news.

The road west out of town quickly narrowed to the jarring double ruts of a wagon trail. Every mile after that, less traveled trails branched off to the north and south. The Union Pacific railway tracks ran alongside for the trail's distance. Here and there were farmsteads, some with sod houses, others with newly built frame houses. Nearly all had grand barns. And not a one was without a windmill, a scattering of scrawny trees, and fine fat chickens strutting in the kitchen yards. In the fifth mile we came upon Harmony School. Harmony, with its daydreaming windows — shattered. Its maps of mountains, deserts, and vast oceans — shredded by the wind. Its desks with sweetheart initials carved in the wood — splintered or removed. Harmony, with a gaping hole in its roof. My eyes hurt from the looking.

Papa mumbled under his breath then, and a moment later I saw what he was mumbling about. There, beside the trail, stood Isaac Bradshaw, skinny as a rail, his cheeks peppered with freckles, and rags tying his shoes to his feet. He tipped his cap to me. I felt my cheeks flush. I smiled and nodded.

Isaac

I STOOD THERE BESIDE THE TRAIL, MY HEART THUMPING AS IF A six-footed rabbit was trapped inside my ribs, and stared after Mr. Barnett's wagon until it disappeared over a rise. Stared until Hannah disappeared over a rise. Hannah with hair the color of midnight. Hannah, who had danced on the prairie. Hannah, the girl who'd saved my sorry life. I was mighty tempted to chase after the wagon, ask Hannah how she'd been faring, but thought better of it. There'd been a warning in Mr. Barnett's scowl — stay away from Hannah or else. So I hog-tied my want and headed for the schoolyard.

The dampness from the grass seeped through the holes in the soles of my shoes, chilling my toes. This put me in mind of something Hannah had said during the blizzard. "Make believe your feet are loaves of bread, hot from the oven." I'd never been one to put much stock in make-believe, but I'd survived when others hadn't, still had my feet and hands when others didn't.

My empty stomach, not knowing the difference between pretend bread and real, begged and growled as I climbed the schoolhouse steps. "Soon," I said, and my stomach shut up. I stopped before going through the door and tried to recollect how many times I'd stood there before. Far too few. Plowing and planting had kept me away every spring. Harvest stretched into late fall. In between there were fences to mend, wood to chop, hogs to butcher, and any other chore my stepfather, Mr. Richards, could dream up so I wouldn't, as he put it, "Get too smart for my britches." If it hadn't been for my ma holding her ground now and again, Mr. Richards would have put a stop to my schooling by the age of nine or ten. As it was, I'd gone whenever I could — a day here, three in a row there.

When I stepped inside the schoolhouse, I half expected Miss Farnham to gawk over the top of her spectacles and frown, half expected the girls to giggle, half expected a spit wad to splat between my eyes. But there wasn't anybody there, only the busted desks, the cannonball stove lying on its side, and a heap of splintered rafters and shingles that'd once been half the roof. At the make-do chalkboard, which was nothing but a plaster wall painted black, I rubbed out "Isaac slept here" with my sleeve and wrote, "Isaac's moving on." That done, I headed for the one dry corner to fetch my gear.

I lifted the moth-eaten wool blanket from the straw pile that had been my bed for nigh onto a week, shook out the dust, and spread the blanket on the floor. Lined up next to the straw pile were my real pa's woodworking tools. I turned each tool over in my hand — block plane, brace, calipers, chisels, and gouges — before laying them on the blanket. The hammer I held for a minute, tightening my grip on the handle that'd been worn smooth by my pa's hand. Next I piled on the few duds that weren't already on my back. The socks, in particular, smelled a little rank. On top of it all, I set my real pa's shoes — good, sturdy shoes that didn't need rags to hold them together.

I folded two corners of the blanket over my gear. I knotted the other two corners in the fashion of a sling, then poked my head and one arm under the knot. The knot resting on my shoulder, leaving my hands free as birds, I set off down the road for Prairie Hill.

Pa's tools clicked and clacked and my shoes flipped and flapped as I hiked along. I pulled my harmonica from my hip pocket, cupped my hands about it, and made up a tune as I kept time with the clack click, flap flip. It was a lively tune, and it got livelier as I stretched out my strides. But when I passed a farmer hunched over a breaking plow, my music slowed to a funeral pace. That farmer had been me six days before.

I'd been busting sod, opening a new field so Mr. Richards could plant some flax. Back and forth, sunup to sundown, trudging through clods and dung, my eyes fixed on the oxen yoke until it felt like the yoke was sawing into *my* shoulders. There wasn't any music in this work, at least none I could hear. Other men heard it. I'd seen it in their eyes when, at the end of a long day, they'd lift a hand to their brow and look out over their land.

I'd tried using Hannah's trick, make believe I was anywhere but in that field, but the only picture that'd come to mind, the only sound I'd heard, was acre after acre, year after year, of lonesome, backbreaking silence. I'd tried again, tunneling deeper into my noggin. Deeper still, and I heard something. A raspy whisper? I reeled the whisper in as if it were a stubborn, bawling calf at the end of a rope. When I'd dragged it close enough, yanked the lasso tight enough to choke, it bellowed, "Is this how you spend your second chance?"

I ran away from Mr. Richards's house that very night, but not before begging my ma to come with me. Her eyes had watered. "Go if you must, but I cannot. My place is with my husband, for better or worse," she'd said. I told her worse was all she had to look forward to, but she only looked away and said there was more to it than I knew.

Ma had smuggled food to me those first days I'd holed up at the schoolhouse, but Mr. Richards must have found her out because there'd been no food for the last three. No matter. I was on my way to a home-cooked meal and a bed that wasn't just an oversized bird's nest.

Down the wagon trail a piece, the click clack, flip flap was joined by another, louder, click clack, flip flap, then louder still and mixed with a belch of locomotive steam. I blew hard into my harmonica, ran my mouth up and down the scale, and then waded through the tall grass that separated the wagon trail from the tracks. Standing as close to the tracks as a fellow dared, I braced myself like a runner about to begin a footrace. The iron horse neared. The earth shivered. Closer still, and I took off, my arms pumping and the tools clacking madly. Double time, triple. The engine edged past. The coal tender. One freight car, then two, then five. Half the caboose. I reached up and into the swirl of sooty wind. Grabbed the bill of my cap. Tipped it just as the caboose sped past. I waited there beside the tracks until I'd caught my wind, then set off again for Prairie Hill.

I smelled the town before I got there. This wasn't altogether disagreeable. Prairie Hill was growing fast — a "boom town," folks called it. There was the spicy stink of the livery stables and street-sweeper's dung heaps, but there were also the stick-to-your-ribs smells of bakeries and eateries and meat markets, the thought of which caused a river of spit to float my tongue.

I heard the town nearly before I got there, too — the metal clang of foundries and blacksmith shops, the echoing thwack of carpenter hammers, the bark of a peddler hawking his wares. It was my kind of music, and I was about to join the band.

The sun was sinking by the time I reached the wooden sidewalk that marked the beginning of Main Street. I sat myself down and fished my pa's shoes out of the blanket. I held one up before putting it on. It threw a shadow of heroic size. Ma had saved the shoes for me, even though it meant Pa'd had to go shoeless into the Hereafter. She'd said they had too much wear left in them to waste. I'd been stingy about wearing them because I didn't want to walk holes in the soles before my feet got big enough to fill them.

I'd learned a thing or two since running away from Mr. Richards's farm, and one of those things was that, to be seen as a young man and not as an ignorant farm boy by the townsfolk, you had to wear decent shoes. I'd been shown the door in several business establishments before getting the chance to apply for a job. The place where I'd most hoped to find work, Boggs Furniture Makers and Undertaking Parlor, was one of them. When Mr. Boggs figured out I wasn't there to buy one of his handcrafted wooden cradles or chifforobes or coffins, he threw me out on my ear, the soles of my shoes flapping.

I'd worn Pa's shoes the next day, and some few of the proprietors had at least let me say my piece. Mr. Hertzel, the wagon maker, had said he'd consider me if I came back in the fall after his boy had started up his studies at the university over in Lincoln. Sons, fathers and sons, was another lesson I'd learned. Establishments with names that ended with "and Sons," as in "Preston and Sons Home Builders," weren't likely to give someone else's son a second look.

I'd finally nailed down a job earlier that day, and in a

most unlikely place. I put my harmonica to my mouth and played my way up Main, past the millinery, dressmakers, druggist, and barbershop. When I got to the corner of Main and Fourth, I stopped and looked up to the north-ernmost window on the second floor of the Ackerman Hotel. That was the room where Ma and I had holed up in the weeks after Pa died. I was a runt of only five, but I remembered, and the thing I remembered most was the bedbugs. I scratched an itch in the middle of my back then played my way around the corner.

A boy, young enough to be wearing knee-high britches, fell in behind me. I switched my tempo to a march, and the one boy was soon joined by two more. They paraded after me as far as the place where the wooden sidewalk veered off to the right. One hollered after me, "Don't go that way. My ma says the Widow Moore is crazy, that likely as not she eats boys for her supper."

"Crazy as a fox," I hollered over my shoulder, then broke into a run. Halfway along, I almost tripped on a loose sidewalk board. I hammered the board flat before moving on.

———————

Before announcing myself to Mrs. Moore, Eliza, I ducked into the stable and climbed the stairs to the sleeping room above to drop off my gear. Eliza had said I was welcome to sleep in the house, but the stable room suited me just fine. It had a cot and a table and two chairs, one of these chairs being overstuffed. *What more could a fellow want?* I thought as I slicked down my hair in the fancy mirror that hung on the wall.

To get to the main house, I didn't have to go back outside. A door on the first floor of the stable led to the room that housed the printing press, where I was to begin working the next morning. From there, a door led into a larger, longer room, which Eliza had said the Judge once used for his courtroom. I didn't know much about courtrooms, but to my way of thinking this longer room said "school." Tall windows lined each of the side walls. At one end the floor was raised to stumble height, like a teacher's platform or a stage. Newfangled gaslights hung here and there on the walls as they did in every room inside the main house, the gas hissing in from wooden pipes that not long before had been dug under the town's streets.

If Eliza hadn't shown me around earlier in the day, knowing which of the room's doors to choose would have been akin to finding the pea in a fast-handed shell game. A door on one side wall opened on the bricked drive. The back yard was gotten to by a door on the other side. Two more doors flanked the raised floor. The first of these led to a room used for washing clothes; the other led to an indoor necessary. Each of these smaller rooms had yet another door, both opening into the kitchen of the main house.

I picked the door to the indoor necessary, thinking

maybe I'd try it out, but sniffed smoke so hurried on through and into the kitchen, where I spied the culprit. I didn't see an oven glove, so I unbuttoned my shirt, wrapped it around my hand, and then yanked the roaster pan out of the oven. Into Eliza's fancy, hung-off-the-wall sink it went, charred chicken and all. My stomach was mighty disappointed.

Hannah

I REMOVED THE PAN OF GOLDEN BROWNED BISCUITS FROM THE oven and then turned to the table where my papa and brothers, their faces and hands freshly scrubbed, had just sat down. Our table wasn't large enough for everyone to eat at once, so the menfolk ate first, followed by Mama and us girls. I served Papa his two biscuits, then Jake, eighteen, and James, eleven, and then moved quickly past the two empty chairs to where Joey sat. Joey looked up and smiled. Joey's was the only smile given in trade for a biscuit. Jake and James wore the same tired expression as Papa.

Hester was dishing up the stew when Joey said, "Hannah took us to a castle."

I froze.

"Hannah," Papa said, "I thought I told you to stop filling the boy's head with your make-believe foolishness."

I'd wanted to wait until after supper to share my news, but Joey had opened the door, so I figured I might as well step through it. I smoothed out the handbill and laid it next to Papa's bowl. "Sir, the castle isn't make-believe, it's a big brick house in town, the home of the Widow Moore, and I applied for a position there today, and she has asked me to return tomorrow morning to stay and work there through the end of the week, and if she finds me acceptable and asks me to stay on, I will bring home every penny of my wage."

Papa picked up the handbill and began to read. Mama wiped her hands on her apron then hurried to look over his shoulder. Hester and Lila's eyes grew to the size of hens' eggs. Jake stuffed his mouth with biscuit; James filled his with stew.

When Papa finished reading, he returned the handbill to the table, took up his spoon, and began to eat. One mouthful, then two, the air in the soddie growing more taut with each lift of his wrist. So taut that, if I waited through another mouthful, I was afraid the air would snap and I would fly apart. I braced myself, hiccupped, then asked, "Do I have your permission, sir?"

Papa took his time swallowing then said, "You told this Moore woman you'd come?"

"Yes, sir."

"Then I'd say it's a little late to be asking my permission."

I should have been relieved, but I wasn't. Papa used a tone meant to hurt, as had become his habit when he was required to speak with me.

Mama returned to the stove, her back to the table, wiping at her apron as if there were something dirty she couldn't get off her hands.

When Papa and the boys had finished their supper and gone out to the barn to tend a sick calf, Mama told my sisters to fill their plates and carry them outside. They didn't fuss. Then it was just me and Mama. Her eyes showed the same worry I'd seen there so many times before — when I'd come home from wandering too long on the prairie. She laid one hand on my shoulder and asked, "Why, Hannah?"

Why? I'd been asking myself the same question, over and over, since the blizzard. *Why* had Jon, Jacob, and I been the only three of my brothers and sisters to wake without scratchy throats that morning? *Why* had the morning air been so deceitfully balmy when the three of us had set out for school — the falling snow so pretty? *Why* hadn't I read the signs in the noontime sky? *Why* had the prairie drawn me in that day? *Why* had I wandered so far? *Why* hadn't I heard the school bell? *Why* had the prairie I'd so loved turned against me? *Why* had I been the only one to ever make it home? *Why?*

"Is it your papa, the way he's been treating you? Is that why you want to go away?"

Again I had no answer. Papa was part of it, the harsh way he often spoke to me, the way his eyes avoided mine. The daily reminder of the two empty chairs was part of it, too. But there was more to it than Papa and empty chairs. I'd been circling the questions like a cat chasing its tail. I knew only one thing. I wouldn't find the answers there in our house. Wouldn't find the answers surrounded on all sides by too much prairie.

"Your papa doesn't blame you, Hannah. Men keep their

grief bottled up inside and once it's in there it gets mixed up and doesn't come out the way they mean it to. And all that talk about you shaming yourself, he doesn't mean that either. You just need to give him more time."

Tears rushed to Mama's eyes then. "And you need to give me more time. I've known from the time you were little that you'd go away from me one day, but I'm nowhere near ready to lose you yet."

"I'm not going far, Mama. Only into Prairie Hill. If Mrs. Moore hires me, I'm sure she will allow me to spend Sundays here with you, and I'm also sure she wouldn't mind if you visited me whenever you are in town."

Mama threw up her hands. "You know yourself how hard it is for me to go into town. There's no decent place to feed the children and all I can think of is the work going undone at home. And, Hannah, have you so easily forgotten the winters when the roads are buried in snow? How many Sundays do you think you'll be able to come home then?"

"I'll find a way, Mama. I promise."

Mama began to weep then, but no tears visited my eyes. I hadn't cried since before the blizzard. When I didn't cry at my brothers' funeral, Hester had accused me of being cold-hearted. She'd been more right than she knew. My heart felt as if it had shattered into a hundred jagged, icy pieces.

Hester, who must have been listening at the window, came into the house just then. She shot me one of her "now you've done it" looks, then guided Mama to her bed and stayed there with her, mumbling comforting words.

Later, after Lila and I had done up the supper dishes and I'd rinsed the mud from my clothes and hung them to dry near the stove, I stuffed a few things into a pillow cover that would serve as my make-do traveling valise. That done, I joined my sisters in our bed. Hester and I, being the oldest, usually slept at either edge. Lila slept in the middle and Megan crosswise at the foot. That night, Hester traded places with Lila. I expected that as soon as Papa had turned out the last of the oil lamps, she'd shame me for multiplying Mama's grief. I turned my face to the sod wall. Megan's breathing fell into sleep, followed in a moment by Lila's. The cornshuck-stuffed mattress tick crackled. I clutched a fold of the quilt. Hester's breath warm in my ear, she whispered, "I'm glad for you."

Her words were like a spring breeze. I rolled over and whispered, "Will Mama ever forgive me?"

"In time."

We whispered then, as we hadn't done for months. Hester wanted to know every detail of my day, how I'd learned of the position, what Mrs. Moore was like, wanted especially to know how I'd been brave enough to rap at her front door.

When Hester ran out of questions, I asked her one. "If suddenly you found yourself quite alone in the world, your only assets a grand house and quickly dwindling funds, what clever, yet tasteful, endeavors might you undertake to support yourself?"

Hester was quick to answer. "I'd take in boarders," she said. Soon after she drifted off to sleep.

An answer to Eliza's question didn't come quickly to me, so I did the thing Papa had earlier said was foolishness. I made believe that I was there in Eliza's house, wearing her ink-stained apron. The carpet tickled my feet as I zigzagged from one side of the main hall to the other, peeking into one room after the other. Books lined the walls of a wood-paneled room; lush ferns decorated another. I stacked logs in all the fireplaces and sun-washed the windows. The kitchen drew me again and again, and I might have lingered there if not for the vision of Mama. Gossamer as a dragon-fly's wing, she stood at the stove, her hands tangled in her apron.

Pulling away from the main house, I next explored the attached, one-story building. Like a ghost, I entered through a wall. The inside was bare. I added roosts and a dozen fat laying hens but removed them when a cocky roos-ter began his wake-the-whole-town crow. Next I nailed shelves to the walls. In a blink, I lined the shelves with dry goods; bolts of muslin and colorful calicos, skeins of yarn, shoes in every style and size, and rocking chairs pulled up to a potbelly stove. Then, quite uninvited, the grumpy clerk from Fowler's Emporium swept in and carted away all my lovely merchandise, leaving behind only the rocking chairs and stove. I imagined myself holding a cup of mint tea, sat down, and rocked — back and forth, the rhythm and creak of the chair like a lullaby. That's when the answer to Eliza's question began to take shape, slowly, like bread rising. I finally fell asleep.

———————

I awoke to the scent of bacon and, to my horror, quite alone in the bed. I moved aside the bed sheet that curtained our corner of the soddie from the rest and shot a glance at the mantel clock. It read nearly six-thirty. Even if I chose to be unladylike and run half the way to town, I'd be late.

Mama came in from outside just then, carrying the morning's collection of cream. Needle-sharp jabs pricked my heart. Separating the cream from freshly drawn milk by straining it through a square of muslin had been one of my chores. Mama didn't look at me, not even when I dashed across the room and gathered up the clothes I'd hung to dry the night before. I'd planned to press these things, but it would take too long to heat and reheat the irons on the stove, so I ducked back behind the curtain and quickly dressed myself in wrinkles.

I was standing at the mirror, brushing out my hair, when the bed sheet fluttered in the draft of the door opening. "I didn't break a one," Joey said.

"How many eggs today?" Mama asked.

"Two hands plus these many fingers."

"That's one more than Megan gathered yesterday. Is Megan nearly finished feeding and watering the chickens?"

"Lila had to help her carry the bucket."

I was almost surprised to see my reflection in the mirror. To Mama I was already gone.

"I'll be home in time for church on Sunday," I said, lifting the door latch.

"Not so quick," Mama said.

I dared not turn to face her.

"If you must go, then at least make yourself presentable." She pinned a hat on my head. I knew the hat without looking. It was Mama's going-to-town hat, the navy one with the floppy silk rose.

"Mind you don't lose my hat," Mama called after me as I set off down the trail toward town.

Papa, Jake, and James were already working in the fields: Papa behind the breaking plow, busting sod like he'd done every day, save for Sundays, since the spring thaw. James was cutting and burning last year's corn stalks, and Jake was sowing timothy grass. Three sets of strong, hard-working hands. Joey would add his hands to the farm work one day, but Papa would forever be four hands short.

When out of sight of the farm, I hiked my skirts and

began to run. I'd been wearing long skirts only since turning fourteen and hadn't yet gotten used to the bother they caused in all but the most mannered of movements. Fine for town living, maybe, but not for getting oneself there.

I made it nearly as far as the schoolhouse before I slowed to a walk. This was partly because I'd winded myself, partly because of a team and wagon stopped in the trail. At first I saw no one about. Then Mr. Richards, Isaac Bradshaw's stepfather, showed himself in the schoolhouse doorway. I hoped he wouldn't see me, but he did. "Wait up," he shouted, then started toward me.

Mr. Richards was not well liked in our district. More than once I'd overheard Papa speak of Mr. Richards's underhanded dealings. A healthy calf offered in trade, then replaced by a sickly one.

"If you've come here to consort with my good-for-nothing stepson, you're wasting your time." His breath reeked of corn liquor.

I took a step back.

"Ungrateful boy robbed me blind before he ran off. Went looking for my woodworking tools this morning and couldn't find hide nor hair of them. You tell him for me that I've just reported him to Sheriff Tulley. Better yet, you're going to tell me where he's hiding out, and I'll make him wish the sheriff got to him first."

I hiccupped, then said, "I'm sorry, sir, but I've not spoken with Isaac in several months. Now you will have to excuse me, for I have pressing business in town."

"That's a likely story," he spat.

I didn't reply, just spun away, hiccupped, and began again to walk toward town.

"You tell him to return my woodworking tools today or else," Mr. Richards shouted after me.

Moments later I heard the crack of Mr. Richards's whip and the hoof beats of his team pulling away. I tried to put Mr. Richards out of my mind but couldn't. I was glad Isaac had run away, glad he'd taken the tools. Mr. Richards's anger worried me, though. I vowed then and there that, if ever I saw Isaac again, I'd go against Papa's wishes and warn him.

Just then there were more hoof beats, coming on, not going away. I chanced a peek over my shoulder and was relieved to see that it was old Mr. Zeller.

He whoaed his team and asked, "Need a lift?"

"I surely do," I answered in my loudest voice, then climbed up and onto the seat next to him. I leaned close to his nearly deaf ear and asked, "How are you faring today?"

"Can't complain," he answered, and that was all the conversation he required.

Isaac

Sleeping on the cot in the room above the stable had been like sleeping on milkweed fluff. No crackle of corn-shucks, no stepbrothers' snores, no bony jabs to my ribs. I slept so good that first night that the sun was already hard at work when my eyes finally pried themselves open. I didn't need to take the time to pull on my trousers because I'd slept in them.

Eliza wasn't in the kitchen and didn't answer when I called her name, so I headed for the print shop. Eliza hadn't been in a mood to discuss the particulars of my job the evening before, or much of anything else for that matter, but she had cursed the press as a "maniacal, mechanical beast."

I approached the press as if it were an unbroken colt — stout-heartedly but with a heap of respect. The press stood twelve hands high and an arms-spread in length. There was a large, chin-high wheel, square plates, one of which held the type, a foot pedal of some sort, and a confusing snarl of gears and arms. At the top was a disk-shaped metal piece, whose purpose I couldn't put a saddle on.

I walked circles around the thing, trying to make sense of its mechanics. If it'd been made of wood, nose to tail, the press might have explained itself, but the forged metal wasn't talking. I snatched a blank sheet of paper from a nearby table, then laid this paper where I thought it might go and gave the wheel a turn. The jaws of the thing clamped shut — quick, like a coyote's fangs sinking into a jackrabbit. I turned some more, and the jaws parted.

The page had printing on only the bottom half. The ink was faint, hard to read; so I walked it over to the window, squinted, and made out one word, *Women*, and part of another, *Suff* —. *Suff* —? *Suffer?* I hightailed it back to the kitchen, where I built a fire in the cookstove. When the kindling blazed, I flung the paper and its "not meant for a fellow's eyes" words into the firebox. It caught, flamed, and turned to smoke.

The charred chicken I'd pieced on the night before hadn't set too well, so I had a bad case of hungries. I snooped in Eliza's pantry and happened across a sack of buckwheat flour. I'd learned a thing or two about cooking in my fifteen years. Had to, what with Ma's sick spells. Flapjacks were my specialty. Mr. Richards, who thought himself and his boys too good for kitchen work, wolfed down platefuls without so much as a howdy-do.

When I opened the icebox, looking for milk, I noticed that the ice block had melted down near to nothing. As I saw it, this was one of the differences between living in town and in the country. On the farm there wasn't a need for fancy iceboxes. You wanted milk; you put your hands to work under a cow. You wanted eggs; you gathered them. You wanted a chicken for supper; you chased one until you caught it.

The eggs looked none too fresh when I cracked them, one-handed, into the crockery bowl. They didn't smell of rot, but I added an extra shake of sugar to the mound of buckwheat flour to be on the safe side. I cooked the same way I worked with wood, by eye. A dollop of this, a pinch of that, a muscled stir.

I wasn't sure if the stove was flapjack hot, so I spat on it. My spit sizzled, did a jig, then disappeared. Excelsior! Then I spooned a puddle of batter into an iron skillet.

"Smells wonderful," Eliza said just as I flipped the half-cooked flapjack in the air. I caught it, returned the skillet to the stove, and then glanced over my shoulder. Eliza's eyes were puffy, her hair was like a haystack, and her dress was about as wrinkled as my trousers. She must have slept in her clothes, too.

"Are you feeling some better this morning?" I asked.

"Much better, thank you. And I'm so sorry about last night; sorry you had to see me like that. I should explain."

I didn't need an explanation because my ma had suffered from spells of the blues, too.

"Hungry?" I asked.

"Starved," Eliza answered.

"This one's almost done."

Soon we were both belly-up to the table, each with a flapjack the size of our plates. "To the success of our partnership," Eliza said, waving her first bite, dripping with butter and maple syrup, like a flag at the end of her fork. I was about to dig in when somebody knocked on the door.

Eliza pushed away from the table.

"You eat," I said, then took my first bite of real food in days. Still chewing, I got up and headed for the door, the one leading outside.

Standing on the other side of the glass was Hannah. I opened the door so fast it sucked wind. I tried to swallow but couldn't. My eyes were fixed on Hannah's, and hers on mine.

"Is that Hannah?" Eliza called from the table.

The bite of flapjack was still stuck in my gullet.

Eliza was behind me then. "Please do come in, Hannah."

Eliza pulled out a chair and asked Hannah to sit. Hannah sat, removed the pin from the funny little hat she was wearing, then removed the hat.

Eliza then asked Hannah if she'd eaten breakfast. Hannah, not taking her eyes off me, answered that she hadn't. The bite of flapjack finally slid down, and straightaway I spooned more batter into the skillet.

Eliza, after fetching another plate, asked, "Do you know one another?"

"Yes, ma'am. We both went to Harmony School," I answered.

Eliza thought a little, then asked, "You're not sweet on each other, are you?"

I kept my mouth shut because I was as anxious to hear Hannah's answer as Eliza was.

"Oh, no, ma'am. If you've heard that, it's not true."

Much as I wished Hannah had said something else, she was mostly right. We'd never been sweethearts, never had the chance to be sweethearts, though rumors to the contrary had been galloping around. Before the blizzard we hadn't even been what one might call friends. Hannah had never been mean to me like the other kids at school. She'd never teased me about my worn-out shoes or being the only fifteen-year-old boy still coming to school. But she'd obeyed her papa like everybody else — "Stay away from that Richards bunch. They're nothing but trouble."

As for me, I'd been sweet on Hannah for as long as I'd been old enough to work a plow. One day, catching a blur off to my right, I'd looked up from the furrow to see Hannah making her way through the knee-high grass. I whoaed the team and gawked. The easy way she moved, the way the wind played in her long, black hair, the way she'd slow and raise her hand to her brow every now again, as if searching for some shining thing in the distance, was music. Hannah music. I scanned the horizon for her whenever I was in the fields. When I didn't see her, the days were mighty long. When luck was on my side, I pulled my harmonica from my pocket and played, softly and matching my notes to the melody of the way she moved.

That's where we'd both been the afternoon the blizzard struck. Mr. Richards had sent me out to round up some cattle that'd busted through the corral fence, and I was about a quarter mile from Harmony School when I saw Hannah. Her head was thrown back as if she were trying to catch snowflakes on her tongue. There was no place for me to hide, what with the dried prairie grass having been laid flat by earlier snows. But she was too busy catching those flakes she didn't see. Then came the clang of the after-lunch school bell. I was sure Hannah would turn and hurry toward the school, spying me, but instead she started walking south. Her eyes were cast down, as if she were following wild critter tracks. I fell in about fifty paces behind her, fitting my feet in her footprints. I stopped when Hannah stopped, walked when she walked, for maybe another quarter-mile.

If we'd had eyes in the back of our heads, we might have seen the storm sneaking up on us and taking aim. As it was, my first clue that something wasn't right was a sparkiness in the air, like a too-close-for-comfort lightning strike but without the jagged white bolt, without the thunder. I looked back over my shoulder and saw the wall of boiling black clouds. "Storm's coming," I shouted. Hannah turned, saw for herself, and then picked up her skirts and began running toward the school. I fell in beside her. We hadn't run far when the wind's fist hit us. Icy, snow-choked wind. Blinding, biting wind. Wind that built a new ankle drift each time we managed a forward step. I was the first to fall. Hannah reached down, found my hand, and pulled me up. "Walk backwards," she shouted close to my ear. That helped some, at least it kept the wind from packing snow in our eyes and up our noses.

We never made it to the school. After what seemed like hours of trudging, my feet so numb they felt like rocks, me falling and Hannah pulling me up, me wanting to rest, Hannah tugging me along, we bumped into a haystack. It wasn't much, but it was enough to keep us alive. Surviving the blizzard, huddled together in that haystack, had turned us into friends. I couldn't ask for more from Hannah than that — for the time being, anyway.

I served up Hannah's flapjack, and all you could hear until we finished eating were our forks click-clacking against our plates. When my plate was empty of all but a dribble of syrup, which I'd have licked clean if there hadn't been women about, I stood up and said, "If you ladies will excuse me, and if I have your permission, Eliza, I'll hitch your filly to the surrey and fetch back a block of ice from the Ice Works."

Eliza wiped the corner of her mouth on a lacy napkin. "That's a capital idea. You'll save us the delivery charge. Take a coin from that tin on the shelf. Hannah and I will tidy up here. And, by the way, the filly's name is Persephone, for the Greek goddess of winter."

I shook a coin from the tin, slipped it into one hip pocket, and slid my harmonica out of the other. I played my way out of the kitchen and into the stable. It was a rip-roaring tune.

Persephone started in whinnying before I'd opened the double, cross-bucked doors. She was a beauty. Coal black and sleek. Not bulky and dull-eyed like Mr. Richards's horses or Mercy, Ma's mule. I tugged on the surrey's tongue, but it didn't budge, so I circled around back to see what the problem was. Wedged in front of the surrey's right rear wheel was an arm-long board. Next to the wheel was a whole stack of boards. And next to the stack hunkered a large lump of a thing, covered by a dust-fuzzed tarpaulin. I lifted a corner of the tarp and saw wood. With a Herculean pull, I yanked the tarp to the floor and beheld the curved wooden spine of a boat.

I didn't stop to think just then about how a half-finished boat had found its way into Eliza's stable. Didn't stop to think why anybody would have such a thing on the Nebraska prairie or why the boat was balanced on an axle and wheels. Didn't think one thing at all, just ran my fingers over perfectly hewn wooden ribs. I guessed the boat's length at half a rod, maybe more, and the width at two people sitting side by side. Unlike the printing press, this contrivance spoke to me. Sang. I might have stayed there, chawing on the possibilities, if not for Persephone. Her whinny had turned into a horsy nag.

I backed away but didn't take my eyes off the boat until I reached Persephone's stall. "Easy girl," I said, taking her halter lead.

When I'd harnessed Persephone, I swung myself up onto the surrey's leather seat. I took up the reins, snapped my wrists with a "Gee haw," and was off. The fringe dangling from the surrey's leather roof swayed and danced as if it were keeping time. My grin was so big I figured it might be stuck that way. And it was, for a couple of hours.

Hannah

I WAS RINSING THE BREAKFAST DISHES, WISHING I'D WARNED
Isaac about my run-in with Mr. Richards. Not knowing
how much Isaac had told Eliza, I hadn't thought it wise to
mention Mr. Richards in her presence. Just then, framed in
the window glass, Isaac drove out of the stable in the most
magnificent of buggies, the most magnificent of horses in
the lead, high stepping and black as night. A winter horse,
indeed. And Isaac, grinning from ear to ear, looked right at
home there in the surrey. This was the life he deserved, and,
much as I wanted it for myself, I wouldn't spoil it for him.

Eliza leaned over my shoulder. "Isn't Persephone a
beauty?"

"Yes, ma'am, she surely is."

"She's a Morgan, a gift from my late husband."

I turned to her. "I'm so sorry for your loss."

Tears rushed her eyes, but her smile didn't fade. "I miss
Harlan terribly. I'll see a man and woman arm in arm . . ."

Mid-sentence Eliza's expression soured. "My Harlan is
gone. Would that I could, I cannot wish him back. But I'll
not conduct myself as if I died with him. I'll not close my
blinds to the sun, will not wear widow's weeds nor veil my
face. Harlan would not expect it of me. He would not. And
I most definitely will not marry another for convenience's

sake, as some of the so-called better class of people in this town have suggested."

I'd never heard a woman speak so strongly, though the way in which Eliza's hands had balled into fists was familiar to me. Then, as quickly as her steam had built, it seeped away. "I'm sorry, Hannah. None of that was meant for you. It's just that the Reverend Cobb paid me a not-so-social call last evening. He threatened that if I don't put an end to my *Women's Gazette*, he'll recommend to the board of deacons that my name be removed from church membership. How dare he? My Harlan donated the monies to build his church. Monies I could surely use just now. But enough of that. Let me show you about, and then you can share your money-making idea with me. You've brought me one, haven't you?"

"Yes, ma'am, I have, but there is something I need to tell you first."

"Oh my, from the look on your face I'm guessing it's something I won't want to hear. Can it wait?"

I nodded.

───────────

Eliza's house was much grander than I'd imagined it. The Judge's wood-paneled library was lined with more books than even I could have made believe. The dining table was large enough to seat my whole family, with chairs to spare. The upper floor housed a second indoor necessary, which was different from the first only in that it contained a claw-footed bathing tub. There were five sleeping rooms, one of which contained everything a small child could dream. Among its furnishings were a crib with faded yellow ribbons woven through the rails, a house for miniature dolls, a wooden rocking horse, and a pint-sized table, set as if for a tea party about to start. Though it was a warm, sunny room, there was something in the air that caused goose bumps to pepper my skin. "My daughter's room" was all Eliza said before quickly returning to the hall.

Eliza apologized for the cellar before we were halfway down the wooden steps. "Dark, dank, place. Gives me the shivering willies." When we got down there, it was clear to me that Eliza had never lived in a sod house. The cellar walls were built of stone. The many windows, though high up, invited light to flood the cement floor. Even the lacy dust webs looked content to be living there. Before we returned to the first floor, Eliza fed a shovel of coal to the belly of the boiler, solving the mystery of the hot water that flowed from the taps.

After I'd seen all there was to see in the main house, Eliza led the way into the one-story structure, which *was* as I'd imagined it. Eliza invited me to sit in one of the two rocking chairs that were pulled up to the cold potbelly stove. She sat in another, then said, "I'm anxious to hear your idea."

"If I were you, ma'am, I'd support myself by turning this space into a resting room for farm women."

Eliza rocked forward. "Tell me more."

"It's hard for farm women to come into town because there's no place for them to bide their time once they've made their trades with the merchants. They must wait in the wagons, sometimes for hours and in all kinds of weather, while their husbands do their business. If they have children, and most do, there's no private place for them to feed or change their babies."

"Are you proposing that I charge a fee for the use of this room?"

"No, ma'am. Charging a fee would never do. Some few farmers have prospered, especially those who have many sons to help work the land. Though most, like my papa, still struggle to make ends meet. Even if there were a penny to spare, farm women wouldn't think to spend it on a comfort for themselves. If the resting room is to make a go, it must be free to all, but not a charity. You will earn your profit by accepting freewill donations — a mold of butter, a pound of home-cured bacon, a jar of chokecherry preserves — in trade for a homey place to wait. That's our way."

"I'm intrigued, but how do we turn butter and bacon into cash?"

"There are a couple of ways you might go about it. First, if you are paid in bacon, you have bacon for your table and save the price of buying it from the butcher. Same with eggs, butter, and the like. Second, if you have more produce than you can eat, you trade the extra at the grocer for the things you need but don't have. Lastly, you might skip the merchants altogether and sell the extra produce to the women here in town. The merchants double, sometimes triple the price between the buying and the selling. If you cut the difference by half, I believe the women of Prairie Hill will form a line at your door."

"How many women do you think would make use of such a place?"

"Prairie County is settled now, all the land taken up. For the most part, there is one farm on each quarter section. Four farms, four farm women, more or less, for every square mile. I've done the arithmetic. The county is twenty-four miles in both its length and width, which multiplies out to 576 miles square. That counts the number of farms, the number of farm women, at something over two thousand. Half might never come, especially those whose husbands don't tarry. Of the other half, some might come only if they need to get out of the weather. But I believe some will come as often as once a month, and others, the ones whose farms are closest to town and those who most crave the companionship of other women, will visit as often as once a week. It might be slow going at first, until word gets out, but once the women know you are here, I truly believe they will come."

Eliza clasped one hand over the other and exclaimed,

"That's what we'll do then, turn this space into a resting room." She leapt from her chair then and began waltzing about the room, pointing out the placement of the furnishings — a chair over there, a sofa here, a table yonder. Isaac would build shelves against one wall, which Eliza would fill with books from her collection, with one shelf saved for the most recent issues of the *Women's Gazette.*

While Eliza chattered I did some imagining of my own. I imagined a blazing fire in the stove. Wood smoke threaded and scented the air. A resting place, safe and warm. If only my brothers had found such a place. If only it had been that simple.

"And I know exactly how we'll spread the word. We'll print handbills, if I can coax my cantankerous printing press back into service, that is. You're the clever one, Hannah. Perhaps you can remedy whatever it is that's ailing the beast."

I followed Eliza into the print shop, where she showed me how the thick ink was applied to the large platen disk. "It's a clamshell letterhead press," Eliza said, fitting a sheet of blank paper on a blotterlike pad. When she set the thing in motion, it printed only half a page. On the page were the words "Ten Reasons Why Women Must Be Granted Suffrage."

"For your gazette?" I asked, trying to hold my brows from creeping up.

"Oh, my yes, this is the blasphemy that Reverend Cobb's in such a dither about. His self-righteous indignation would be better served if he rousted one or two of his male parishioners from Shipman's Saloon and Billiard Parlor."

My brows stayed in place, but the corners of my mouth curled into a smile. Shipman's Saloon and Billiard Parlor was responsible for none too few of the wagon-waits farm women had been made to suffer. My papa had said his own visits to Shipman's were necessary because much of the town's business was conducted within its walls, which were single-storied behind a false two-storied front.

As for the matter of suffrage, I chose not to comment because I hadn't given it much thought. Papa had. I'd once heard him say from behind his newspaper that if women got the vote it would crumble the foundations of the American home. Mama, who'd been darning a hole in his sock, peered over the top of her spectacles and quietly replied, "Don't see that it'd make much difference around here. When you live in a sod house, crumble is about all you've got." If Papa heard, he didn't let on.

"Try it again," I said, crouching so I could watch the workings of the press's many arms and gears.

"And again."

On the third try, I spied the problem. A bolt had worked itself loose from an arm. I asked Eliza if she had a wrench. She answered that she wouldn't know a wrench from a plow blade, then fetched the Judge's toolbox. And finely forged tools they were, with wrenches of every size. I removed the one I thought would best fit the job, then tightened the bolt to the arm as firmly as I could.

"Once again," I said. That time, when Eliza set the beast in motion, the arm didn't jerk to the side.

Eliza plucked the page from the press and passed it to me. "We're in business. See here, the page printed perfectly."

The ink was damp, but the letters were as crisp as the notes of a meadowlark's song. Words, sentences, neatly arranged thoughts — a thing to be reckoned with. Before the ink had dried on the first, Eliza had printed a second and a third. A thought multiplied. Eliza stepped away from the press. "Needless to say, your trial period is over. I'd like you to stay on permanently."

I focused my eyes on the floor. "I'm honored, ma'am, but I cannot accept your offer. That's what I wanted to tell you earlier."

"Nonsense, you must stay. I wouldn't be able to manage the resting room without you."

I wanted to tell her the truth, that my papa would never approve of my living and working in the same house as Isaac.

"I'm needed at home."

"It's me being here, isn't it? I'm the reason you've told Eliza you can't stay."

I spun toward the door, where Isaac was standing.

"Oh, no. It's not you. I truly am needed at home."

Isaac strode toward me, stopping only when his face was inches from my own. He smelled of leather and fresh air. "Then why did I find this pillow cover stuffed with your belongings on the kitchen stoop?"

I hiccupped.

"Is there something I should know?" Eliza asked.

"Yes, ma'am, there is," Isaac answered.

Isaac

COME SATURDAY NIGHT, HANNAH'S RESTING ROOM WAS READY. In ones, twos, and threes, depending on the heft of a piece, we'd toted furnishings from the house to the resting room. I'd have set these things down any old way, but not Eliza. We'd place a piece of furniture against a wall, Eliza would stand back, look hard, then say it wasn't right, and we'd drag it across the room only to have her decide the first way was better. Almost every room in the house had taken a hit in Eliza's hunt. The parlor was minus its velvet settee, the front hall its parson's bench, and the Judge's study its mahogany library table, which Eliza had said was old and rickety. Rickety, my eye. The tabletop didn't have a scratch, and its legs were as stout as a lumberjack's.

Getting the word out about the resting room was the only thing that still needed to be done, and that's what Hannah and Eliza were fixing to do that Sunday morning. Seeing as how Eliza didn't feel welcome in the Reverend Cobb's church, and seeing as how Hannah was planning to spend the day at home, Eliza had asked if she might tag along, meet Hannah's family, and, as she'd said, "discreetly distribute" handbills to the ladies at Hannah's church.

Before they rode off in the surrey, I'd begged a favor of Hannah: If she could get my ma alone after church, would she tell her my whereabouts? Hannah had said she would try.

I spent most all of the day with my nose buried in a boat-building book I'd found in the judge's library. It was head-scratching complicated — the soaking and bending of boards, the watertight caulking. But, along about dark, I put the book aside and headed outdoors, which had become my habit. Lying low in daylight and going out only after dark, like an owl or a raccoon, had solved a couple of problems.

The first problem being Sheriff Tulley. He'd come to Eliza's door not three hours after I'd returned from the Ice Works, saying that there was a thief on the loose, a thief who played the harmonica, a thief by the name of Isaac Bradshaw. Seems the sheriff had been asking folks around town if they'd seen me, and the proprietor of the Ice Works had told him a suspicious-looking boy had been seen driving Eliza's surrey. Lucky for me, I'd been in the print shop when the sheriff had come nosing around, so I'd heard the story secondhand. Eliza had twisted the truth and told the sheriff that she'd hired a boy to go for ice that morning, but that the boy had made himself scarce soon after.

After the sheriff left, she'd come straight to me and said, "If I were in your shoes, I'd seek out the sheriff and tell him my side of the story. And I'd do it today."

I couldn't do that. It would've been Mr. Richards's word against mine. I knew which side of that coin would land face-up. On the short side of things, I'd have to turn over my pa's tools. On the long side, the sheriff would lock me up in his jail. Losing my freedom, only a few rooster crows after gaining it, wasn't the way I wanted to spend my second chance.

In a roundabout way, my lying low had fixed Hannah's problem, too. Hannah's pa had forbidden her to be *seen* with me in public. If I weren't *seen*, Hannah would be free to stay. Hannah, who could be as stubborn as a thistle root, had kept on claiming that she'd have to leave, that bending her pa's true meaning didn't make it right, and if she were caught that would only make matters worse. Eliza had been the one to sway her. "After all you've been through, you've earned the right to make up your own mind," she'd said, then reminded Hannah of the good that was to be done by the resting room, adding that the women might not come if one of their own wasn't there to make them feel welcome.

I was some worried about Eliza and Hannah being on the road after dark that Sunday evening, so I shimmied up one of the taller trees on Eliza's property. When I'd climbed to the highest branch that held my weight, I straddled a limb and stared out across the prairie in the direction of the westerly road. There was only a hangnail of a moon, and, try as I might, my eyes couldn't split the dark. Leaning my back against the trunk, I bided my time with a little of Hannah's make-believe. The tree was the mast of a sailing ship, a ship bound for far-off shores. I was the first mate, keeping watch for other ships passing in the night. Little did I know that my make-believe was about to turn real.

I heard the wagon before I saw it — the clank of the doubletree rings, the creak of the wagon box, the snuffled complaints of tired horses. These sounds didn't come from the street, but from the prairie to the back of Eliza's property. As the wagon got closer, I was able to make out its odd shape. Most traveling wagons were topped with canvas, but the top of this wagon looked to be all wood.

The driver halted the team not fifty feet from my tree, then jumped down from the seat. He leaned a tiny ladder at the back and opened a skinny door. Three children climbed out. The oldest girl, who looked close to Hannah's age, headed straightaway for Eliza's well and began to pump water into a bucket. The father tended to the horses, wiping the day's sweat from first one then the other's coat. The younger children, a boy and a girl, made a beeline to the woodpile, where they scooped up armloads of kindling, which the father later used to build a campfire. Both the clothes the family wore and the language they spoke were foreign. I knew it was rude to spy, but someone had to keep an eye on Eliza's property. I was more than happy to oblige.

There was much going in and out of the wagon, much rattling of pans, and before long, smoky food smells rose from the stovepipe chimney that poked through the wagon's roof. My stomach let out a growl. It'd been a couple of hours since I'd wolfed down the last of the leftover pot roast. Hungry as I was, I didn't want to give myself away, so I stayed put even though the wind had picked up and was threatening to roust me from my roost.

The food was cooked inside the wagon but was eaten in the light of the campfire. The mother ladled something that looked like stew into bowls. Good-smelling stew, spicy. To keep my stomach from growling louder than it already was, I switched my attention to the wagon. The wagon walls were crusted with woodcarvings — scrolls and curlicues and fretwork — like my pa had fashioned for homes in Bismarck, North Dakota, before our train trip south. Perched there in that tree, I couldn't help but think how different things might've turned out if we'd made our journey in a wagon like that, moseying along, eating Ma's cooking, stopping to rest every night.

The train had sickened Pa from the start. The rocking motion, the babies bawling, the stifling heat of having the windows closed, the choking smoke and cinders of having the windows opened, had heaped up on Pa like the weight of a blizzard's drift. We'd been headed for the Gulf Coast of Texas, which Pa had said was about as far from North Dakota winters as we could get. We weren't halfway along when Pa's heart gave out. His hand had flown to his chest.

The color had drained from his face. He'd gasped and slumped forward, and by the time the train whistled the next stop, Prairie Hill, my pa was dead.

When the family below had finished their supper, the father took out his fiddle and began to play — lively music, of a kind I'd never heard before. My foot set itself to tapping the air, and pretty soon my harmonica was in my mouth. I wasn't planning to give it any wind, but I got so caught up in the music that I didn't even notice when the fiddle music stopped.

"Who goes there?" the father called up from under my tree.

I about jumped out of my skin and had to grab a branch to keep my balance. I didn't fall, but my harmonica did. Fell and fell. Catching the downwind in its reeds and making a gaspy, heart-hurting sound. Then, just before it smashed to the ground, the man caught it. I'd already given myself away, so there was nothing left for me to do but climb on down.

Lucky for me, Eliza stepped out of the shadows just then. "So good to see you again, Mr. Tinka," she said, sticking out her hand, which Mr. Tinka didn't shake like I thought he would. He kissed it!

Eliza then introduced me to the family. She rattled off their names, but I only caught one, the oldest girl, Rosa.

Her name fit her look. Rosy cheeks, dark eyes. Not as pretty as Hannah — no girl was as pretty as Hannah — but pretty all the same.

I leaned over to Eliza and asked, "Where's Hannah?"

"She's in the stable, unharnessing Persephone. I wanted to help her, but she stubbornly insisted that I come on ahead."

I made tracks, but by the time I got to the stable, Hannah was already forking hay into Persephone's stall. I plucked the lantern from the hook on the stable wall and brought it close to Hannah's face so I could read her look. Her look said, "bushed."

I told her as much and suggested that maybe she should just go on up to bed.

"I don't want to disappoint Eliza," she answered. "She is anxious for me to meet her friends."

So we joined the others around the campfire.

Mr. Tinka came up to me then, his fiddle and bow tucked under his arm. "Play," he said, offering up my harmonica. I was about to tell him I didn't dare when Eliza said, "There's a bit of chill to the air tonight. The townsfolk will have their windows closed, and the sheriff lives way over on the other side of town. Your choice, but I think it's safe."

"After you," I said to Mr. Tinka.

He drew his bow across the strings and began to play. I

listened for a bit, to catch the rhythm, then put my harmonica to my mouth and joined in, making up my part as I went along. Before long, Rosa began to dance around the fire. One arm above her head, the other across her waist, fingers clicking in time. Then Mrs. Tinka and the young ones started in dancing, too. Eliza, who'd been swaying along with the music, threw up her hands and said, "Oh, why not," and then joined the others, leaving Hannah the only one not letting the music move her. Eliza tried to fix that. She sashayed over to where Hannah stood and took up one of her hands. Hannah did take a couple of steps forward, did begin move in a way that wasn't quite a dance but wasn't scarecrow-stiff either. The fire's glow lit Hannah's face, and I thought I saw a flicker of the old Hannah in her eyes. But the flicker didn't last. All of a sudden, Hannah jerked away from Eliza and headed, half running, half stumbling, for the house. I bolted after her.

Hannah

WHEN ISAAC CAUGHT UP TO ME ON THE STAIRS, HIS FACE WAS the picture of concern. I tried to reassure him that I wasn't troubled, only in need of sleep, like he'd said earlier. This was partly true. It had been a long and troubling day: Mama apologizing to Eliza for the state of her housekeeping, the simpleness of the meal; Papa turning his back when I offered him the three-dollar wage Eliza had so generously given me; Hester and Lila so full of questions; a Sabbath spent telling half-truths so as not to reveal that Isaac and I were working together, living in the same house.

"There's no sin in having a little fun," Isaac said.

"My brothers aren't having any fun, are they?" I was sorry as soon as I said that, sorry for snapping at the one person who understood, the one person who would never snap back. I locked my heart against any but friendlike feelings toward Isaac, took his hand and squeezed it. I turned away from him then and finished climbing the stairs. I was afraid he'd follow, or maybe I hoped he'd follow, but he didn't, and soon the fiddle playing began anew — soft and slow as a kitten's purr.

In my room, I settled on the floor at the base of the window. Rosa, keeping time to the slower tempo, danced in a less frenzied way. Arms raised, head thrown back, she swayed and dipped as if a ribbon caught up in a gentle wind. I couldn't bear to watch, to remember the times I'd moved my own body in a similar way, so I turned my attention to Isaac. Campfire shadows played on his face and lighted his eyes. The lock on my heart fell away, and I felt the same warm feeling I'd felt when we'd held each other during the blizzard, a feeling no decent girl should have when her brothers are dying. Shame was my bed partner that night.

When I woke the next morning the Tinkas were gone. I was sorry for this because I'd wanted to apologize for my rude behavior of the night before. Over breakfast, Eliza shared that the Tinkas were travelers, never staying long in one place, in part because their different ways often made them unwelcome, in part because they preferred the freedom of their way of life.

After breakfast, Eliza set off for Main Street, a stack of handbills tucked into her market basket. Isaac headed straightaway for the print shop, where he began to prepare the press for the latest edition of the *Women's Gazette*.

I divided my time that morning between the resting room and Eliza's laundry. Monday also being wash day for most farm women, I'd cautioned Eliza not to be disappointed if no one came.

Doing up the wash at Eliza's was no work at all because Eliza had the most modern of washing machines. The boiling water, soap flakes, soiled clothing, and linens went into a footed tub, attached to which was a levered arm I simply cranked a hundred times back and forth. Isaac's socks were a challenge, though. They smelled so bad I had to run them through the wash three times.

After pegging Isaac's wet things to a line in the cellar, I was carrying the laundry basket to the clothesline in the back yard when hoof beats clattered the brick drive. I hurried into and through the resting room, reaching the drive-side door just as old Mr. Zeller was helping his wife, Flossy, down from the wagon. Before he went on about his business, Mr. Zeller gave Flossy a peck on the cheek.

I showed Flossy around the resting room, pointing out the bookshelves, the stack of gazettes, and the indoor necessary, where she excused herself. While she was otherwise occupied, I tapped a warning signal on the door leading to the print shop. Three taps meant there were visitors about, that Isaac shouldn't show his face or work the press. Two taps meant the coast was clear. A single tap meant that Isaac should unlatch the door and let Eliza or myself inside.

When Flossy came out of the indoor necessary, she smiled and said, "Never thought I'd live long enough to use one of those. Sure would come in handy in the winter, wouldn't it?"

"Yes, ma'am, very handy."

"Would it be okay if I helped myself to one of those rocker chairs?"

"Of course. Think of the resting room as your home away from home."

When Flossy was seated, she removed her knitting from the cloth bag she always carried. "Figured I might as well bring my work with me," she said, her needles rat-a-tatting.

"Is there anything else I can do to make your stay more comfortable?" I asked.

"Thank you, but I have everything I need. Now you go on about your chores. I'll not have you fussing over me."

I excused myself and returned to my laundry basket. Eliza joined me just as I'd pegged the last of the wash to the line. She nearly broke into a run when I told her our first visitor had arrived. In the resting room, we found Flossy still in the rocking chair, her chin resting on her chest, fast asleep, though her nap didn't last long.

"Yoo hoo," a woman's voice called.

Eliza and I spun around. A smartly dressed woman stood just inside the door.

"Good day, Mrs. Callahan," Eliza said in a tight voice. "To what do I owe the honor of your visit?"

"I read your handbill down at Fowler's Emporium, and I thought I'd stop by to ask if the ladies of the Betterment Society might be of help. I'd offer to help you myself, but my sister, who lives in one of the finest neighborhoods in Philadelphia, has taken ill, and I'm leaving on the first train out tomorrow."

"That's a very generous offer, but I don't think we'll need any assistance at this time. Hannah here is my partner, and she's done a wonderful job."

Mrs. Callahan looked me up and down, but her eyes didn't stay on me for long. The bustle beneath her skirts bobbing with each step she took, she headed for the bookshelves. When she tilted her head to read the titles, her wide-brimmed, feathered hat nearly toppled. And when her eyes landed on the stack of gazettes, she didn't waste any time snatching one up. "Is there a charge?" she asked, turning to Eliza.

"Ten cents, as is clearly printed in bold type."

"Oh, dear, I'm afraid I left home without my coin purse. I'll just take this with me and send my daughter, Drucilla, over with the price later today."

Just then a thump echoed from behind the print shop door. Mrs. Callahan's eyes swiveled to that direction. Eliza and I traded glances. "You will have to excuse us now. We have much work to do," Eliza said.

With a rustle of skirts, and a humph, Mrs. Callahan went on her way.

When all that remained of Mrs. Callahan was the too-sweet scent of her toilet water, Eliza turned to me and whispered, "She's a meddler and a gossip. If my guess is right, she's on her way to the Reverend Cobb's with my blasphemous gazette this very moment."

I'd set much of the type for the gazette and hadn't seen anything I couldn't have said or thought in a church. No vile words, no threat of evil. New ways for women to think about their lives, maybe, but nothing immoral or scandalous.

Flossy laid her knitting in her lap. "Must be something pretty interesting in that paper. May I buy one?"

"It's free to you," Eliza said. "A gift for being our first visitor."

———

Lunch that day, and all the days after, was eaten in the print shop. So as not to raise suspicion, Eliza and I took turns carrying our plates through the resting room from the kitchen, a spare plate hidden beneath a heaping one. The food was divided in the safety of the print shop. That way, Isaac, whose stomach was like a bottomless well, ate three quarters of the food on my plate and three quarters of Eliza's as well.

The afternoon brought but three more visitors. The first was a Mrs. Randolph who told us she'd arrived from England only the week before. Her daughter, who couldn't have been much more than two, toddled over to Eliza and held up her arms. Eliza picked her up and gently brushed the little girl's hair away from her eyes. "And what might your name be?" Eliza asked.

"Rebecca," the little girl answered. Then, pride glowing in her cheeks, she added, "I rode a train."

"Is that so? Well, how would like to ride a wooden horse?"

Rebecca clapped her hands together and squealed.

"Wait here, then," Eliza said, putting the child down. "I'll go fetch the handsome steed from his corral."

While Eliza was off on her errand, Mrs. Randolph asked me if it might be possible to heat water for "a spot of tea." I told her that I'd see to it right away and headed for the kitchen.

I rekindled the fire in the cookstove before filling the copper teakettle from the hot water spigot at Eliza's sink. While the kettle was filling I happened to look out the window. Isaac's mother, a shawl draped over her shoulders, rode by on the back of a mule. I set the kettle on the stove and then went out to greet her.

"Is he here?" she asked after I'd helped her down from the mule.

"I'll take you to him," I answered. In the stable, I tied the mule's lead to a hitching post, then rapped a signal on the door leading to the print shop. The door opened a crack, and one of Isaac's eyes peeked out. "Ma," he said, flinging the door wide.

"Why don't you and your mother go up to your room, where you can visit without being overheard," I whispered.

"Thank you, Hannah," Isaac's mother said. "You are a dear."

Together they began to climb the stairs. "Does he know you've come to town?" Isaac asked.

"Oh, no," his mother answered. "I was up before dawn, got the wash on the line, made his lunch ahead, and told him some of the church ladies were holding a meeting."

I couldn't help but smile. Isaac's mother was nearly as skilled at telling half-truths as I was. Ladies, church-going ladies most likely, were indeed meeting — in the resting room.

When I passed through the resting room, little Rebecca was merrily rocking on a wooden horse — the very same rocking horse I'd seen in the nursery on the second floor.

By the time I returned to the kitchen, Eliza was emptying the copper teakettle into a gleaming silver one. Arranged on a matching tray was a fancy tea service — cups, sugar bowl and creamer, dainty spoons.

"These things are too fine," I said.

"Nonsense. Fine things are worthless unless they're shared. Harlan's mother taught me that. When she first took me in I . . . uh . . . off with you now, before the water loses its heat."

I carried the tray and my questions into the resting

room, and Mrs. Randolph exclaimed, "I feel like a commoner invited to tea at Queen Victoria's court."

"Everyone is equal here in the resting room," Eliza said from over my shoulder. "This is a place where all women may come to rest and enjoy the company of other women."

Then came another "Yoo hoo" at the door, though from a younger voice than in the morning. I turned, and there was a girl in yellow, from the color of her hair down to the satin of her shoes. Eliza, recognizing her as Mrs. Callahan's daughter, Drucilla, said, "May I help you?" in a polite though guarded voice.

"My mother has asked me to return this," Drucilla said, holding out a crumpled copy of the gazette.

I stood close enough to Eliza to see that many of the passages had been marked through with ink and that handwritten notes had been scrawled in the margins.

Drucilla turned to leave then turned back. "Did you mean what you said, that all women are welcome here?"

"Young and old, town and country."

"I overheard my mother telling the Reverend Cobb's wife that you have books here, sitting right out in the open for anyone to read. I was wondering if that might include me?"

"Your mother wouldn't approve, would she?"

"No, ma'am. But I believe I'm of an age where the choice should be mine."

"What age might that be?"

"Seventeen last Wednesday, ma'am."

"You're right. You are old enough to decide things for yourself. You're welcome to read whatever you like."

"Do you have any works of Shelley or Keats?"

"Several volumes of each, but before you get lost in their poetry, I'd like to introduce you to Hannah. She's my partner here in the resting room."

I smiled and stepped forward. Drucilla, who before the day was out would ask me to call her Dru, smiled back. Dru, who would become my bosom friend.

PART II

Mid-July, 1888

Isaac

By mid-July, three leather-bound guest books had been scrawled with the names of visitors to the resting room. Most of the women arrived on foot, others by wagon, and a few of the younger and more daring galloped up the drive on horseback. I'd seen just two of these visitors face to face. The others I'd only glimpsed in their comings and goings from behind the curtained window in my room above the stable or heard as a group mumble through the print shop walls.

Ma had visited as often as she dared, though she'd kept her visits short for fear Mr. Richards would find out that she wasn't in whatever place she'd told him she'd be. When she arrived, Ma would always say, "Let me feast my eyes on you," then walk a circle around me like she was making sure I hadn't lost any of my parts or grown any new ones. After she'd done that, she'd start in fussing about how peaked I looked. "Pale as flour paste," she'd say, shaking her head, then unload the gifts she'd smuggled out from under Mr. Richards's nose by tucking them into secret pockets she'd sewn inside her skirts. One day it'd be a half-loaf of her raisin bread, another a few strips of jerked beef. Always, just before leaving, she'd peck a kiss on my cheek like she'd done when I was little boy.

Only once had she done something different. It was as hot as a blacksmith shop in my room that day, so Ma and I whisper-talked down in the stable. We were sitting in the boat, which, according to Eliza, had been a hobby for the Judge — a reminder of boyhood days spent sailing off Cape Cod. A boat Eliza had said was mine for the keeping if I finished her. Ma and I sat there in the near dark, side to side.

"Make believe you are on a ship, Ma, the wind strong in her sails," I said after a longer than usual quiet.

"Where might I be sailing off to?" Ma asked, her voice as lively as a girl's.

"Away from Mr. Richards," I answered.

"Please don't say things like that, Isaac. I'm his wife, and I'm beholden to him."

"You owe him nothing."

"But I do. I should have told you this before: he's the one who paid for your pa's plot in the cemetery. He's the one who paid our boarding bill at the Ackerman Hotel. There we were, without a penny to our name and about to be thrown out on the street with no place to go and no family to ask for help, when he raps on the door to our room and says right out that his wife's just died and his boys need a ma and the undertaker's told him of the fix we're in and will I marry him, all in the same breath. I wanted to slam the door in his face, but I didn't, though before I agreed to marry him I made him promise that he'd let you get your schooling."

A knot had tightened like a fist in my gut. "How much did we owe, Ma?"

"Nearly eighty dollars."

"You've paid him back a hundred times, Ma. Slaving in his kitchen, putting up with his foul mouth."

"Enough," Ma said. "Let's not spoil our time together fretting over that which can't be undone. I want to use the little time I have left to talk about a thing that can be undone. You can't go on like this, son, holed up here like a bat in a cave. It's not natural for a body to live like this, not healthy, and I'm begging you to give Mr. Richards the tools so he'll drop the charges against you and you'll be free to live your life out in the open as God intended."

"I can't do that, Ma. You know I can't."

"All I know is that your health is more important than those tools. Holding on to them isn't worth it, Isaac, and Mr. Richards will never give up looking for you, because he knows the law is on his side. The tools rightly belong to him now. When we married, everything that was mine legally became his."

I didn't answer Ma back, just asked her to wait and then leapt over the side of the boat and hurried into the print shop to fetch a handful of old issues of the *Women's Gazette*.

When I got back, I helped Ma down from the boat and gave her the papers. "Read these, Ma. Eliza and others like her all over the country are trying to change things for women, trying to change the laws."

Ma tucked the papers into one of her secret pockets, and

she never asked me to return the tools again, though the next time she came to visit, and after she'd taken her scissors to my shaggy hair, she did go sneaking off to talk to Eliza. Don't know exactly what Ma said, but later that evening Eliza offered to telegraph an old friend of the Judge and ask on my behalf if he might have a job for me. Seemed this man owned a fleet of tugs and barges on the Mississippi. I told Eliza that unless she wasn't happy with my work I'd rather stay. What I didn't tell Eliza or Ma or even Hannah was that when and if I did leave I wasn't planning to leave alone.

The other visitor I'd seen face to face was Drucilla, Dru. Her ma being away and a hired girl doing all the housework, Dru came to the resting room every day except for Sunday, which was the only day her banker pa was home to notice if she was there or not.

Dru discovered me not long after her first visit. I was working in the print shop, quietly stuffing gazettes into envelopes and writing the addresses on the outside, when there came a single rap on the door. I undid the latch, then posted myself in such a way as to be out of sight when the door opened. Dru peeked in. When she saw me she grinned like she was about to tag me "it." Without thinking, I grabbed her arm, jerked her inside, and slammed the door closed behind her. It was kind of like reeling in a fish then not knowing what to do with it once it was landed. I just stood there, dumbstruck and gawking.

"You had best close your mouth before a swallow builds a nest," Dru said.

Still I stood there, saying nothing and wishing I were wearing Pa's shoes.

"You're the boy the sheriff is looking for, aren't you? Well, you needn't worry about me. My lips are sealed." Dru raised a hand to her lips and turned a make-believe key.

"Visitors aren't . . . aren't allowed back here."

"Oh, I'm no visitor. I'm Drucilla Callahan, though you may call me Dru."

"How did . . . did you know the signal?" I fumbled.

"I figured it out by watching Eliza and Hannah. One rap and the door opened, like magic. I love a mystery, and there are none to be found in this town, save for in Eliza's novels — and now for you. Tell me everything — how long you've been hiding out here, what dastardly crimes you've committed."

Another single knock at the door. Hannah. When she saw Dru and me standing there, toe to toe, the skin on her forehead puckered.

"I'm sorry, Hannah. I simply couldn't bear to wait another minute to learn who you were keeping hidden away behind the door. But you needn't worry — I'll not tell a soul." Dru then moseyed across the room and started tinkering with the press. "So this is where the blasphemous *Women's Gazette* is printed. Isaac, that's your name, isn't it? Will you show me how it works?"

"Maybe another time," Hannah said just as I'd started across the room. "The young ones are begging for another of your stories, Dru."

"My audience awaits." Dru breezed past and then was gone.

I was about to say that Dru was really something when I caught myself. She *was* really something, but I sure didn't want Hannah to get the wrong idea, so I said, "I . . . uh . . . do you think we can trust her?"

"I think so, but I'll talk to her, make sure she understands the trouble we'll both be in if you are found out."

And then Hannah was gone, too, and the print shop felt twice, no a hundred times as empty as it'd ever felt before.

———————

After the resting room closed for the day, Hannah and I told Dru our story, the same one we'd told Eliza, leaving out the same part, about spending the night together in the haystack. I might have told that part, too, if it'd been just me, but I was afraid the telling would be too hard for Hannah. I'd hoped time would fix things for Hannah, hoped I could fix things for Hannah, but time hadn't and I hadn't. She went about her days, play-acting that everything was fine when she wasn't fine at all.

Hannah was her bluest after her Sunday visits home. I suggested, once, that maybe she shouldn't go, that she should spend her Sunday with me. "I promised Mama, and this is one promise I will keep," she said before turning on her heel and heading out the door.

Sundays were the best days for me. And the worst. The best because, as long as I stayed indoors, I had free run of the house, resting room, and stable. Sometimes I did just that, ran. From stable to attic, up the stairs and down, over and again until I thought my lungs would cave in. Sometimes I'd tunnel under a pile of quilts and play my harmonica. Always I worked on my boat. The boat had become a friend I could tell my troubles to. The boat knew the whole of my and Hannah's story.

And Sundays were the worst of days because there was no Hannah. No Eliza, who visited a different country church every Sunday. No Dru gushing over how like a character in a novel I was or reading me flowery passages from poetry books or pestering me to read the part of Shakespeare's Romeo to her Juliet. No hope of Ma stopping by. No group mumble, company of sorts, drifting out of the resting room. Only me and my silent boat.

Before the blizzard, I hadn't minded being by my lonesome, preferred it if truth be told, but the boy who crawled into the haystack wasn't the same boy who crawled out.

Hannah

A CHILD FIRST TAKES A WOBBLY STEP, THEN TODDLES, THEN walks, then runs. So it was for the resting room. By mid-July, the resting room had found its balance. Wednesdays and Saturdays were "Market Days," days when the town women, market baskets over their arms, came to purchase eggs, butter, preserves, or freshly rendered lard; homespun wool yarn, tatted lace, rag rugs, or bed-sized quilts, to name but a few of the items Eliza and I had arranged for display.

Many of these market goods had been left by visitors as their freewill donation. The other items, especially the more valuable like the quilts and crocheted tablecloths, had been left with us on consignment. Often was the time Eliza had to suggest an asking price because many of the women didn't know the value of their own handiwork. Eliza then added a small percentage to cover our time in tending to the sale in the woman's absence. Always was the price of the items less than that charged by the merchants on Main Street. Always was the quality higher. Always was the smile on the woman's face beaming when she next returned to the resting room and Eliza counted out her earnings.

The number of gazettes we mailed to women all over the country had remained about the same, but the circulation in and around Prairie Hill had grown from nearly nil to well over three hundred per week. This increase was due in large part to the page of social happenings we inserted in the local copies — weddings, births, country church socials, and the like — items that had been reported to us by women visiting the resting room. Paid advertisements had increased from exactly zero to five or six a week — Maggie's Millinery and The Sisters Trimble Dressmaking Shoppe being two of these. The front page, as before, contained articles Eliza had written or articles sent to her by like-minded women in the East. In setting the type, which gave me plenty of time to think about what the words meant, I was beginning to understand why Eliza was so passionate about changing things, especially when it came to articles about the awful working conditions of children, some as young as my sister Megan. Boys in West Virginia coal mines, girls in Massachusetts textile mills. One such headline read, "Lincoln Freed the Slaves — Who Will Free the Children?"

Mama had visited the resting room the Wednesday after it opened, Joey and Megan in tow. "Had to see for myself that this is a safe and wholesome place," she'd whispered. Her stay was brief because she didn't want to keep Papa waiting, though Eliza did manage to send her off with several issues of the gazette. I had no idea that Mama had read them until the day she surprised me with a second visit. She'd come into town not with Papa but with the Zellers. Most surprising, she had left all the children at home. Mama discussed with Eliza the price she should charge for her cross-stitched gingham aprons, then asked if I could spare a few minutes from my work for a private word in my room. Madeline Moore's watchful portrait eyes seemed to follow us as we passed down the main hall and started up the stairs.

Once we were sitting on the edge of my bed, Mama turned to me and said, "I've been reading those gazettes, and what's in them is fine and good, for grown women, city women, but you're little more than a girl, Hannah. Promise me that this is as far away from me as you're planning to go, at least until you're old enough to know your own mind."

"You needn't worry, Mama. I'm perfectly content here at Eliza's."

"You've never been content, Hannah. You've been moving away from me, moving toward some faraway place ever since you began to crawl. And worrying is what mothers do. You'll know what I mean when you have children of your own. Now, I've got to have your promise, Hannah."

"I promise this is as far as I'll go, Mama." I hadn't given a moment's thought to moving on, but, once made, the promise felt like a too-small and scratchy wool coat.

My promise tucked up her sleeve like a handkerchief, Mama was full of chatter. Papa had finished planting the corn, her snap beans were coming up, Lila had broken one of her best teacups. It was the first time in my memory that I'd had Mama all to myself for more than just a few minutes, and I paid extra attention to the strands of gray that laced her dark hair, the garden scent of her, the warmth that filled the space between us, so I could imagine her into my room whenever I was lonely for her.

After a bit, Mama ran out of homey news and shifted her talk back to me. "What kind of a life do you imagine for yourself, when you're grown, that is?"

If she had asked me this question before the blizzard, I might have answered that my dream was to set off walking and not stop until I'd called out my name from a mountain peak, danced circles in a dense forest, and wet my feet in an ocean. That dream being dead and buried, I gave Mama the safe answer — that I hoped to marry a fine young man. I ached to tell her that Isaac Bradshaw might be that young man. Ached to ask her if she thought Papa would ever approve. But I knew I couldn't and Papa wouldn't.

Papa had also begun coming to Eliza's. He'd pull his wagon into the drive, drop off Mama or Hester or Lila and the goods meant for the market. When he returned, I'd bring him a glass of ice water, and if there was a strawberry pie or chiffon cake or other delicacy among that day's freewill donations, I'd offer my share to Papa. His stomach seeming to be in greater need of feeding than his pride, he never turned me down. Thinking that perhaps he was softening toward me, I'd once slipped a dollar from my wages in with the money Mama had earned from the market, but

Papa, with his quick mind for numbers, saw that the item-by-item receipt didn't add up. He thrust the dollar back at me and then drove off. One step forward, two back. I hadn't tried that particular trick again, but I was still saving my money, hoping for that day in the future when Papa was ready to accept my wage, ready to forgive.

I'd spent only twenty cents of my savings on myself — for two months' dues in the Working Girls Social Club. Though the club met Wednesday evenings in the resting room, I chose to pay my way like the others. There were nine of us, all farm girls working for families in town. The idea of it came about one market day. Inga Swenson, who worked for Doctor Forbes and his family, had been sent by Mrs. Forbes to fetch back a pint of cream and mold of butter. After making her purchase, Inga took me aside and asked if the resting room might ever be open to visitors in the evenings.

"Is there a need?" I asked.

"Oh, yes. I've made the acquaintance of other working girls, but there's no place for decent young women to socialize. Our employers don't allow us to invite visitors to our rooms, not even on Wednesday evenings, which besides Sundays is the only time we're free to do as we please."

Working girls. Working girls with a need. Maybe not as great a need as the girls in Eliza's articles, but a need all the same. And I could help. So without even thinking to ask

Eliza's permission first, I boldly declared, "Spread the word — from now on the resting room will be open to working girls every Wednesday evening."

When I did tell Eliza at the end of the day, she said it was a splendid idea and that she was proud of me. But I wasn't very proud of myself when I rapped the all-clear signal on the print shop door. In my eagerness to please Inga, to please myself, I'd narrowed Isaac's freedom by one evening a week.

I told Isaac of the thing I'd done in one breath and promised to undo it with the next. "You'll do no such thing," he said, grinning big. "What red-blooded fellow wouldn't give up a little freedom for the chance to be a wall away from a room full of girls?"

I thought something then, felt something I had no right to think or feel. Jealousy leaves a sour taste in the mouth, and I was afraid Isaac might sniff it on my breath. "You've become quite the ladies' man, haven't you?"

Isaac stuffed his hands in his pockets. His Adam's apple bobbed up and down with his swallow. "Naw. There's only one girl for me. I think you know her. Her name's spelled the same forw—"

My hand flew up and covered Isaac's mouth. I don't know what I was going to say then, but something, because I knew if Isaac finished his sentence everything would change, change as surely and permanently as it had after the blizzard. I'd have to stop pretending that we were just friends, that living and working in the same house with the boy *I* was sweet on wasn't indecent. Have to stop pretending, pack my things, and go home. But I never got so much as a word out because I started in hiccupping, one right after the other and so loud that they carried all the way into the resting room. "Are you all right?" Eliza asked, rushing in.

I didn't even try to answer.

"We'd better get you into the kitchen. Garlic's what you need. It always does the trick for me."

———————

The garlic Eliza mashed and told me to hold on my tongue didn't stop my hiccups, nor did her second choice of a cure, gulping cider vinegar. Her remedies only made me reek. Isaac's remedies didn't work either, though they were easier to swallow — dill first, then dried bread, then a spoonful of clover honey.

So I was sitting there at the kitchen table, hiccupping hopelessly, when Isaac rubbed his chin and, with the most sober of voices, said, "I heard tell of a man who hiccupped himself to death. Eliza, do you reckon I should go out to the stable and start building a coffin?"

"'Tis a pity, but perhaps you should."

They later told me that I was so startled I nearly fell off my chair. But my hiccups were cured, and I'd kept Isaac from saying my name.

"Something happened here yesterday after I left," Dru said not five minutes after arriving the next morning. "Some tiff between you and Isaac. I can tell by the way you two are avoiding each other's eyes."

"It was nothing, just my foolishness."

"There's a story here, and I'll not stop pestering you until I've heard every detail."

In hopes of turning Dru's attention in a new direction, I said, "I have news. The working girls here in town will be coming to the resting room every Wednesday evening."

"May I come?" Dru asked.

Eliza joined us then. "Only if you finally agree to accept a wage for all the work you do around here."

"I should be the one paying you. Being here has spared me from a summer cinched into my corset unable to breathe properly. And I've learned so many things I otherwise wouldn't have learned."

It was true, Dru was a tireless worker, pitching in wherever there was a need, be it helping with the laundry or changing a toddler's nappy while a young mother was occupied with a nursing infant. She was especially gracious when serving tea, though her true gift was in her storytelling. She was so good the children often shrieked when she told scary parts. As for the corset, when Dru had learned that Eliza didn't wear one, thought them harmful to a woman's health,

Dru had stopped wearing hers, too. I'd never worn a corset myself. Being poor had its advantages.

"Will you at least accept a token wage?" Eliza asked.

Dru smiled. "The least amount that will qualify me as a working girl. Could you see your way clear to a penny a day?"

"A penny it is then."

"And might I invite Clarice, Mother's hired girl? Though I've tried to befriend her, she is very shy and will only give me a nod. Perhaps meeting with the other working girls will bring her out."

"By all means, invite Clarice and all the girls who work for your mother's friends," Eliza said.

Needless to say, Dru's penny wage always found its way into the freewill donation tin.

Dru held herself back during the first meetings. She sat quietly and listened as the girls told amusing stories about mistakes in etiquette they'd made or charming things the children in their charge had said. It was only when the girls had become better acquainted that their conversations began to circle around the conditions under which some were made to work. Cass, who was seventeen and from a farm to the north of town, worked for a mistress so particular that if a garment or table linen was not ironed to perfection, the mistress would grab it away, crumple it, then require Cass to press the piece again. Mary, who was eighteen, was unhappy that she wasn't allowed to entertain her fiancé, not even on her employer's front porch in broad daylight. Sadie, who was sixteen and the youngest save for me, had the worst of it. She was made to sleep in the same bed with a four-year-old boy who wet the sheets, and then she was assigned the blame for not waking the boy every hour throughout the night. All the girls had unpleasant stories to share — Inga and Carol, Imogene and Gertrude. All the girls save for Clarice, who accompanied Dru to the resting room each Wednesday evening. She smiled politely but spoke only with a nod.

I said little myself, having no unpleasant stories to share. I did listen, did sympathize, but more often than not my thoughts fell on Isaac locked away behind the print shop door.

Eliza made herself scarce during the Working Girls Social Club meetings. She spent the time in the print shop with Isaac, writing articles for the next edition of the gazette or, alongside Isaac, working the press. I knew this was a sacrifice on her part, knew she'd have loved nothing more than to join in the girl talk.

We'd been meeting for about a month when, during a lull in the conversation, Dru finally spoke up. "What we need is a purpose."

"What sort of purpose?" Inga asked.

"Oh, I don't know, something to throw ourselves into, keep our minds off our troubles."

"And what troubles might you have?" Carol chimed in.

"Oh, I didn't mean to imply——"

I jumped in before Dru could finish. "Dru's right. We should always make time for those who need to talk, but that shouldn't be our only reason for getting together. You all have talents — perhaps we should think of ways to put them to good use."

"A pageant," Dru said. "We should have ourselves an end-of-the-summer pageant, right here in the resting room — invite the families you work for, your families at home. It'll be grand."

Several girls groaned, but it was Mary who spoke first, "Might we invite our beaus?"

Eliza, who had come out of the print room to see what all the excited voices were about, pulled up a chair, sat down, and said, "I think a pageant is a splendid idea, and you may count on my assistance, if assistance is required. And yes, if you have beaus, by all means invite them."

"Are there any plays among your books?" Clarice asked Eliza. It was the first time we'd heard her speak. Her voice was lovely.

"Greek tragedies and Shakespeare, of course, but might

it be more satisfying if you wrote a play of your own? One that speaks to your lives in this time and place?"

"Yes, exactly," Dru said, "and there is one among us who can write it." Dru then turned to me. "Hannah, you are the one who can make magic with your make-believe. You must write the script for our play."

"Oh, no. I couldn't possibly. You are the storyteller. It should be you."

"But I can only retell stories I've already read, not make them up new."

Clarice tugged at my sleeve. "Please write a role for me." Her cheeks glowed.

How could I say no to that? "I can't promise, but I'll give it a try."

"Three cheers for Hannah," Dru said, and when the cheer went up I heard Isaac's voice join in with the others.

Isaac

ELIZA, IN A RUSH TO FIND OUT WHY THE WORKING GIRLS WERE making such a ruckus, had left the print shop door ajar. I was about to ease it closed when I heard Dru say, "Three cheers for Hannah." I couldn't help but join in. Soon after came the all-clear rap, and I opened the door to Hannah. "I heard you," she scolded.

"Did the others?"

"I can't be sure, though no one turned an ear. You must be more careful, else you'll find yourself in a place even more confining than this."

"What about you were we cheering?"

Hannah stared at the floor. "They'll not be cheering when next we meet and learn that I have no talent for writing a play."

"A play!"

Hannah looked up and said, "Yes, a play, and I don't have a clue where I'd even begin."

"You were always good at those dramatic readings you gave at school."

"Reading is one thing, writing quite another."

"If you'd be willing to go for a walk with me, the fresh air might clear your head."

"I'm not sure a walk tonight is wise. The moon's so bright it's nearly like daylight out there."

That was closer to a "Yes, I'll go for a night-walk with you" than I'd gotten from Hannah since the day I'd stupidly set off her hiccupping spell. Only an even stupider fellow would let moss grow on a second chance like that. "Breathing in a little of that moonlight might be just the thing to stir up your make-believe, and we can hold to the shadows."

"Well, maybe just this once."

———

We left the gaslights burning in the resting room because Eliza and Persephone would soon return after driving home the girls who worked on the far side of town. We'd just passed the woodpile when I saw something out of the corner of my eye. Quick as a lightning bug's flash, I covered Hannah's mouth with one hand and pulled her to the ground behind the woodpile with the other. Hannah peeled my hand away. "What is it?" she whispered.

I craned my neck and looked over the top of the wood-pile. A man moved in the shadows near the stable not a stone's throw from where we crouched. *Mr. Richards*, I thought, reaching for the handle of an axe wedged in one of the logs. The man passed in front of the window light, and then it was Hannah yanking me down. "It's Sheriff Tulley," she whispered close to my ear. I let go of the handle and squeezed my hand over hers. Hannah squeezed back.

The next time I looked, Sheriff Tulley was inside the resting room. He passed by one window, then the next, and then he must have opened the door to the print shop because the paper covering the windows lit up.

"What do you think he's looking for?" Hannah asked.

"Me. One of the girls must have heard me cheering and turned me in."

"How could that be? Even if one of them did hear, they'd have no way of knowing it was you."

"Dru knows."

"She wouldn't turn you in. You know that as well as I."

"I suppose, but if he's not looking for me, why is the sheriff here, sniffing around?"

"I don't know, but I think it's best if I go in there, distract him before he discovers that someone has been living above the stable." Hannah pulled free of my hand just as Sheriff Tulley came back outside.

I ducked. Hannah stood up.

"Good evening, sir. May I help you?"

"Who goes there?"

"Hannah Barnett, sir. I work for the Widow Moore."

"And what might you be doing behind the woodpile at this late hour? Is there a young fellow back there with you?"

I wanted to ram my fist down his throat.

Hannah hefted a log from the pile. "Oh, no, sir. I'm fetching wood for the morning fire." She circled around then, out of my sight. "If you wish to speak with the Widow Moore, I expect her return any minute now."

Hannah's voice was as solid as a rock. It was as if she'd just stepped to the front of the school and begun a dramatic reading.

The sheriff followed Hannah into the resting room and shut the door behind him. I shot across the lawn and crouched under the window closest to the door.

I listened hard but could only make out mumbles, so I inched my head upward until I could see into the room. Hannah headed to the corner where the market goods were stored. The sheriff followed, and when he got to the table, he started digging through the pretties like a dog in loose dirt. A couple of things fell to the floor, and Hannah picked them up. Still the sheriff dug, then, as if finding the bone he'd been digging for, he held up a red shawl and said something to Hannah. Hannah nodded, and the sheriff removed what looked to be a coin purse from his vest pocket, opened it, and dropped one coin in Hannah's upturned hand. He dropped another, then another, then still more before Hannah finally took her hand away.

It wasn't long before I felt the thud of the drive-side door slamming shut. Then, one by one, the gaslights went out, and not long after that Hannah was at the back door.

"Over here," I whispered.

"Follow me," she said, then hiked up her skirts and commenced to run across the lawn at breakneck speed, stopping a few paces short of the prairie, where she flung herself down on the grass. I offered her a hand up, but she brushed my hand aside. "Join me."

I wasn't about to argue with that, and we both lay there, staring up at the shiny moon. Fireflies flickered. Crickets chirruped. A warmish breeze carrying the sweetness of prairie grass blew across us.

"I've done a terrible thing," Hannah said after a time, then giggled.

I propped myself up on an elbow and looked down at her. "It can't be all that terrible if it makes you laugh."

"I don't know what came over me."

"Tell me."

"Okay. The sheriff wasn't looking for you at all. He came to buy the knitted red shawl Flossy Zeller left with us on consignment. Mrs. Tulley was here earlier today, admiring the shawl. I overheard her telling Eliza that the weekly household allowance her husband gives her doesn't stretch far enough to buy nice things for herself. Eliza sent her home with a copy of the *Women's Gazette.* You remember the one, with the article listing the value of each household chore, the money a husband would be required to pay someone else if not for the free labor of his wife and children."

I remembered, full well. Charwoman, laundress, cook, and all the chores my ma slaved over for Mr. Richards. I'd summed it up. If he'd hired her instead of marrying her, the debt Ma owed Mr. Richards would've been paid before the first year was out. "The sheriff's wife must have read the article, raised a stink."

"Seems so," Hannah said. "And an expensive stink at that. I charged him more than Flossy's asking price. I know that was wicked of me, but there he was, talking big of licenses Eliza supposedly failed to obtain, threatening to close the resting room. And all the while he was saying those things, what he was really after was the shawl. He thought because I'm young and nothing but hired help that he'd scare me into selling him the shawl cheap. And it might have worked if not for the fact that he'd tucked only half of his nightshirt into his trousers, part of the tail trailing out."

Hannah exploded with laughter then. Real laughter, not girl giggles, and I laughed right along with her, long and hard until I thought my sides would split. When we finally wound down, I sucked in a breath and asked, "Exactly how much did you charge?"

"Double," Hannah answered, and our laughing started up again.

I might have stayed there all night, sprawled in the sweet-smelling grass, staring up into the starry sky, making believe that Hannah was my girl and I was her beau. But it didn't last. Life wasn't make-believe, and Eliza had finally returned.

We picked ourselves up out and hurried across the lawn. Eliza was fumbling with Persephone's harness. Even in the dim light I saw that her eyes were red and puffy. "Let me," I said.

She turned away and headed for the house.

"She's been to the cemetery again," Hannah whispered.

I nodded, then led Persephone to her stall.

Hannah

SLEEP DIDN'T COME EASY THE NIGHT OF SHERIFF TULLEY'S VISIT. At first my thoughts were too tangled with the sounds carrying down the hallway from the nursery room — Eliza, humming lullabies and then crying. There was a pattern to Eliza's grief. I didn't always know what set it off, but I knew where it took her — the cemetery, followed by hours behind the closed door of her daughter's room. She spoke often of the Judge but never of her daughter. I didn't question why one but not the other because of something I'd overheard Mama say to Hester after my brothers' funeral: when a mother loses a child, instead of the other way around like it's supposed to be, the world is turned upside down.

Later, after Eliza had retired to her own bedroom, my thoughts were tangled in the play. I scolded myself for allowing Dru to turn my head with her flattery. I didn't want to disappoint the other girls, especially shy Clarice, so I decided that the very least I could do was try. I tossed and turned, discarding one silly idea after the other. I'd nearly given up when, as I was lying there staring across the room and out the window, the curtains riffled in a sudden though pleasant breeze. The curtains billowed out then in, as if a living, breathing thing. The seed of an idea took root, and I finally closed my eyes and slept.

The sun was bright at my window when I awoke the morning after the sheriff's visit — too bright. And I wasn't the only one in the house who had overslept. When, after hurriedly dressing, I passed along the hall, I saw that Eliza was still in her bed. Imagining a line of women waiting at the resting room door, my feet landed on only every other of the stair steps. It wasn't until I threw open the door between the laundry and the resting room that I slowed for a breath.

Dru, an apron covering her lilac-colored dress, was sitting on a tufted footstool and reading a story to a young guest. The child's mother was sweeping the floor. Another woman was emptying the contents of her basket onto the freewill donation table — a Mason jar of preserved beef, a mess of string beans, and a sumptuous-looking rhubarb pie. No lunch would need to be prepared that day, nor, for that matter, dinner. Yet another woman was sitting at the quilt frame, her needle gliding in and out. The resting room had begun to run itself.

Mrs. Farley, one of our most frequent visitors, arrived just then and immediately sought me out. "I've brought Rusty along with me today. Where should he begin?"

Rusty — Russell, as was his given name — was the youngest of the eight Farley sons. Mrs. Farley paid her way at the resting room and bought her weekly copy of the gazette with Rusty's hard work. He mowed Eliza's lawn, pruned the shrubbery, chopped wood, did whatever outdoor chores needed to be done. He'd once offered to muck out Persephone's stall, but Eliza had declared the stable off-limits.

Rusty, grinning from ear to ear, appeared at the door just then, tipped his cap, showing his curly red hair, and said, "Good morning, Hannah. Should I start with the lawn?"

"The lawn it is," I answered, then glanced at Dru. I'd hoped Dru hadn't noticed Rusty's arrival. Dru, who, like a red-tailed hawk, missed little, returned a wink, and I knew I was in for a teasing later.

Dru was convinced that Rusty agreed to accompany his mother and work so hard because he was sweet on me. I'd seen Rusty looking my way a time or two, his shoulders squared and his smile denting his dimples. Rusty was a fine young man, as handsome and sturdy as the finest wool, just the kind of fellow Papa would have gladly given permission to call on me when I was a bit older. I might have encouraged Rusty's attention if not for Isaac. Compared to Rusty, Isaac was silk. I'd never worn silk, probably never would, but I was used to doing without.

I wasn't the only one Dru teased about Rusty. She was fond of telling Isaac of Rusty's supposed interest in me. Every time she mentioned Rusty's name, the skin on Isaac's ears and nose, so badly frostbitten by the blizzard, turned radish red and the cords in his neck stood out.

After Rusty had gone on about his business that morning, Mrs. Farley asked, "Is Eliza about?"

"She's otherwise occupied just now."

Mrs. Farley creased her brow. "I hope she has not forgotten that we are meeting at ten o'clock this morning to discuss the upcoming council elections."

"I'm sure she hasn't forgotten."

The council Mrs. Farley was referring to was the Resting Room Advisory Council. Eliza had asked a handful of the more regular visitors to serve. At their first meeting, the women had made a list of "Courtesies." Eliza's only rule was this — Every woman, regardless of family circumstance, nationality, or creed, will be welcomed and shown the highest and equal regard. To this, the council, after much debate, had added: Leave the resting room as tidy as you found it; Children must be tended at all times; News is welcome — hurtful gossip is not.

The councilwomen took their responsibility quite seriously. More than once I'd overheard one or the other of them ask a visitor how the resting room might better serve their needs. That's how the curtained area for nursing mothers and the installation of the quilting frame came about. The frame, donated by an older woman whose hands were so arthritic she could no longer work a needle, was a blessing for those not accustomed to resting their hands. One would bring in a pieced quilt top, stretch it in the frame, and the next time she returned, the tedious quilting might be complete. Sometimes women came to town, to the resting room, for no other reason than to sit at the frame and, while quilting, chat. On the busiest days, walking a circle around the quilting frame, one might hear three or four languages being spoken — English, of course, but also Swedish, Russian, and German.

An election of council members was to be held in the fall. Eliza expected that most of the current council members would, as she'd said, "throw their bonnets in the ring." Privately, Eliza had shared with me her hope that the election would help the women to see that taking a more active role in decisions that affected their and their children's lives would not lead to the ruination of hearth and home as so many politicians, and "none too few husbands," had led them to believe.

I was chatting with Mrs. Farley, asking after her ill mother's health, when Megan and Joey burst through the door, followed by Hester. I excused myself from Mrs. Farley and hurried over to greet them. "I lost a toof," Megan said though a new gap in her smile.

"I've got a penny," Joey chimed in. "Papa said I do my chores good. Said I can buy a peppermint stick."

Megan and Joey then made a beeline for Dru, whom they called the "Story Lady."

"Let's step outside," Hester whispered. "I have something I need to tell you that I don't want others to overhear."

Rusty mowed himself around the corner just as Hester and I stepped out onto the lawn. He tipped his hat, showing his mop of red hair. I nodded.

"Who's that?" Hester asked, her eyes following Rusty's path.

"The son of one of the councilwomen. But tell me, what's the news you've brought me? Is something wrong at home?"

"How old is he?" By then Hester's head was swiveled almost backward.

"Seventeen," I answered. "But enough of that. Tell me your news."

"News?"

"Hester!"

She finally turned to face me again. "Oh. Yes. It's that Bradshaw boy, Isaac. He's still in the county. Has been seen sneaking about after dark, and nearly every farmer in our district, when checking their stock of hand tools, has reported finding at least one missing. Mrs. Kramer swears she heard him one night, breaking into her kitchen, and that the next morning one of her sharpest butcher knives was gone."

"Don't believe everything you hear, Hester. Isaac wouldn't do such things. Believe me on that."

"It's true, Hannah. People have seen him. I shiver to think that you once spent the night in a haystack with that wild boy." Hester then lowered her voice to a whisper. "There are those who say something bad happened to you that night, something you're ashamed to tell, and that's why you've run off to work here in town. Is it true, Hannah? Did Isaac shame you?"

I choked back a scream that was building and boiling and burning in my throat. "Yes, something bad happened that night — my brothers died and I did not. I wasn't in the school like I was supposed to be, wasn't with them like I should have been, and they died. That's the awful truth. The beginning and end of it. Isaac did nothing except keep me warm, keep me alive. How many times must I tell the story before I'm believed? How many times before you believe? You can't begin to imagine the horror."

Tears sprang to Hester's eyes. "You're right, Hannah. I can't begin to imagine."

The idea for the play that had come to me on the evening breeze rooted itself. Deep. I would put an end to the rumors, remove the smudge from Isaac's name, once and for all, help Hester and the others to see. And I would begin at once, painful as I feared the writing might be.

And I did begin, later that morning. Eliza had appeared, chipper and clear eyed, at precisely ten o'clock and sat down with the councilwomen. Not wanting to interrupt, I asked Dru to pass on a message that I'd be spending the rest of the day in my room.

Dru's bottom lip pretended a pout. "I'd hoped we might put our heads together today, come up with an idea for the play."

"I'm sorry, Dru, but the play is something I want, no, something I *need* to do by myself."

"You have an idea, then?"

"I do."

Dru's eyes danced. "Will there be a role for me, a very dramatic one? A tragic figure, like Shakespeare's Juliet, where I choose death if I cannot be with my truest love? Or a dastardly villain? Oh, yes, I've always wanted to play a villain!"

"There will be tragic and villainous figures enough to go around," I answered, then headed for my room.

Isaac

THE MORNING AFTER THE TULLEY SCARE, NEITHER HANNAH
nor Eliza had shown their faces at breakfast. I'd waited in
the kitchen as long as I'd dared, then locked myself up in the
print shop only minutes before Dru arrived. Dru had
rapped on the door and asked through the wood why neither Hannah nor Eliza were about. Before I could tell her I
didn't know, a visitor arrived and I was left to wonder by my
lonesome. I thought maybe they'd eaten some rancid food.
But I'd eaten the same boiled tongue they'd eaten the night
before. Then I thought maybe someone had broken into the
main house and hurt them. I kicked myself for not having
had the guts to go up to their rooms, whether they were still
in their nightclothes or not.

I tried to keep my mind on my work, but that was like
trying to keep my mind on fresh-baked bread while tromp-
ing through a barnyard of manure. The walls of the print
shop squeezed closer, the ceiling lower, than ever before.
Then I'd heard the sound of the mower moving back and
forth. Rusty Farley! And the print shop shrank until it
wasn't any bigger than the burrowed space at the center of a
haystack.

I raced up to my room, where I spied on Rusty out the
window. The morning sun threw a tall, manly shadow and
shone on his tanned, muscle-thick arms. I felt about as

small as Joey, who, with his sisters, happened just then to pass below the window.

I kicked at one of the legs of my cot, forgetting that I wasn't wearing shoes. I grabbed that foot to rub it, all the while hopping up and down on the other foot. All this rubbing and hopping caused me to get off kilter. I whacked my head on the corner of the cot on the way down and wrenched my shoulder when I hit the floor. I lay there, staring at the ceiling rafters, thinking how much they looked like the bars of a critter cage, then picked myself up and limped down to the stable.

Persephone snuffled. "Don't bother me," I growled, then headed for the rear cross-bucked doors. I listened for Rusty and his mower, reckoning his coming toward and going away. Then, when I guessed Rusty rounding the corner from back lawn to front, I shot through the doors and ran. Twenty paces, forty, like chasing a train, then a dive into the prairie grass. I lay there, my chest heaving, and stared up into the bluest sky. Blue and wide and deep like an ocean.

Hannah's make-believe was easy there in the grass. The earth against my back felt like the ribs of my boat. I fixed the clouds in place so it seemed like I was the one drifting, not them. I got so lost in the idea of it that I caught myself reaching for the oars.

Then I heard voices, and the clouds broke loose and

started sailing across the sky again. I sat up and parted the grass just enough so I could see who it was but not enough so whoever it was could see me. Turned out to be Hannah and Hester, and Hannah looked fine, not sick or hurt. If my relief had been a tree, it would have pulled up its roots and danced a jig. But the jigging didn't last for long, because about then Rusty mowed himself back around the corner of the house. Seeing Hannah and Hester, he tipped his hat. Hannah nodded. After that, Rusty strutted like a rooster and the swath he cut in the grass was as crooked as a snake's.

I couldn't stomach looking at Rusty any more than I already had, so I turned my attention back to Hannah, and my earlier relief lost all its leaves. I couldn't make out what Hannah was saying, but the wild way she was flinging her hands told me she wasn't swapping recipes. Something was wrong. No doubt about it. And I was as trapped outside as I'd been in.

Not long after that, Hannah and Hester went back inside and I was left watching Rusty. Back and forth, stopping every now and again to wipe his forehead on the sleeve of his shirt. I thought he'd never finish, and when he did the sun was noon-high and blistering. I'd left the stable without my cap, and the sun was singeing the tops of my ears, frying my nose, turning me the color of Russell Farley's hair.

Thinking the coast clear, I was about to race back to the stable when three women, trailed by a passel of young ones, marched out of the resting room. They settled in the shade of the walnut tree and commenced to eat their lunch.

The next person to show herself was Dru. She peeked behind the woodpile, knuckled the door of the outside necessary house, and shot upward glances into the trees. I uprooted a hank of prairie grass, shook some clods of dirt loose from the roots, and then lofted a clod in Dru's direction. The clod fell short. I lofted another and another until Dru jerked her head in the direction of my hiding place. She started toward me, but then one of the women under the tree said something, and Dru skedaddled it back to the resting room. And then I figured I was really sunk. Until Eliza showed up.

She strode from the stable door, pushing the wheelbarrow I always used, late at night, to dispose of Persephone's dung. The wheelbarrow was heaped high and covered by burlap feed sacks. After trading nods with the women under the tree, Eliza wheeled the barrow in a path the pitchfork handle, like an accusing finger, pointed out.

"Isaac?" she whispered.

I rustled a clump of grass.

"I won't ask why, that's your business, but I do think it best for all our sakes if you return to the house."

"You won't get an argument from me."

Eliza threw off the burlap sacks and forked, which stirred up the stink. Her nostrils curled, but she kept at it until the barrow was empty.

"Climb in," she said, holding one of the burlap sacks as a curtain between the women and me.

I didn't have to be told twice.

"Make yourself as flat as you can," Eliza said, covering me with the burlap. Eliza gave a not-so-girlish grunt when she heaved the handles up and set the barrow to rolling. "Lovely day," Eliza called out to the women on the lawn.

Under the burlap, I was gagging.

In the stable, I didn't waste any time getting out of the barrow. Eliza didn't waste any time, either. She picked up an oak bucket, dipped it in Persephone's water trough, and then dumped it over my head. "Don't move," she said, dipping again.

Eliza was about to douse me a third time when Dru showed up. "May I?" Dru asked.

Eliza handed Dru the bucket. "Be my guest."

"This is for the fright you gave me," Dru said, letting go.

Then Eliza said, "If you two will excuse me, I think I'll go for a stroll, air myself out a bit before returning to the resting room."

When she was gone, I turned to Dru. "I saw Hannah

before, talking with Hester. Her hands were buzzing around like bumble bees, like she was mad or scared or something."

"She's gone up to her room."

"In the middle of the day! Now I know there's something wrong. If only I could get to her, see if there's something I can do to help."

"Go to her as a friend, right?"

"A friend, sure. One friend helping out another."

Dru grinned. "Then I have an idea that might work. Go change out of those putrid, sopping clothes."

Back in my room, I stripped down to my skin and then washed myself all over with the same basin water I'd used for a spit bath earlier that morning. I could've used a soak in Eliza's fancy bathing tub, but I couldn't get to that either.

I'd just finished toweling off when Dru banged on the door. "Are you decent?"

"No," I answered, wrapping the towel around my waist just in case Dru took a notion to barge in anyway. With Dru you never knew.

"Hide yourself behind the door then, and I'll slip this bundle inside. And I know what you're going to think when you see what I've brought, but it's the only way. I'll wait here on the landing, in case you need any help."

The door creaked open, a pile of clothing plopped to the floor, and then the door creaked shut. A gingham bonnet topped the pile. Under the bonnet was a worn-over pair of women's high-button shoes, and under the shoes was a raggedy brown dress. Dru had raided the Betterment Society castoff box her ma's friends had left in the resting room. Until that day, not one thing had ever left the box.

"You don't expect me to wear these . . . these . . ."

"How badly do you want to see Hannah?" Dru asked from the other side of the closed door.

I didn't answer.

"They're just a fabric covering, not skin," Dru said. "You'll not change into a woman. I promise you that. For centuries men have taken the roles of women in the theater. Simply think of it as play-acting."

I held up the dress and tried to twist my mind around so I could see it the way Dru saw it. A covering, nothing more, nothing less. I put on a clean pair of trousers, then showed the mirror my backside and pulled the dress over my head. "Not skin," I said to myself as I reached around to do up the buttons. I did manage to fit one button into a hole but missed the mark and the button was two holes too high.

"I could use that help now," I said to the door.

Dru breezed in. "Having a little trouble with the buttons, are we?"

"Why do they sew them to the back?"

"Use your imagination. What if the buttons run down

the front and one pulls open or pops, what might then be seen?"

"Oh."

"It's a good thing you're so skinny, else I'd have to cinch you into a corset."

"Oh."

Dru dragged the bonnet over my sunburned ears and tied a girlish bow under my chin. "Now for the shoes."

I sat on the cot and tried to shove my feet into the shoes, but my feet were too thick.

"I was afraid of that," Dru said. "We girls are made to wear narrow shoes from little on, so our feet are forced to take on this shape. The hem of your dress touches the floor, so I don't think anyone will notice if you wear your own shoes underneath."

There was that to be grateful for. In my pa's shoes, at least my *feet* would feel like they belonged to a man.

When Dru had finished her fluffing and declared me "lovely," we headed down the stairs to the stable. We had a plan. Dru would go out first, make sure there were no women close enough to get a good gawk at me, then I would, as Dru had said, stroll, taking birdlike steps and swaying my hips, past the resting room and enter the house through the kitchen. It was a mighty fine plan, but it never saw daylight.

No sooner had we reached the bottom of the steps than the stable doors flew open, letting in the Tinka wagon. I yanked the bonnet off my head, and stood there, dumbfounded. Eliza, who'd been the one to open the doors, rushed over to where Dru and I stood. "The Tinka boy has been shot. Dru, go at once and fetch the doctor." Then, as if not noticing that I was wearing a dress, she said, "And Isaac, you tend to the Tinkas' horses."

Dru, her skirts hiked to her knees, left at a run. I didn't bother with the buttons, just ripped the dress away and let it fall in a heap to the cobblestone floor, and then straightaway I began to unhitch the team. Leaning back and looking sideways, I saw Mr. Tinka come down from the wagon, his boy, Carlos, in his arms. Carlos was limp, his shirt soaked with blood.

"Up there," Eliza said, pointing to my room. Mrs. Tinka, the lap of her dress stained red, hurried after. Eliza, holding the hand of the younger girl, followed Mrs. Tinka up the stairs.

Rosa still hadn't shown herself by the time I finished with the horses, so I circled around to the back of the wagon and looked in. Rosa sat on a mattress on the floor, her face in her hands, her body rocking back and forth.

Hannah was at my side then. "What happened?" she asked.

"Carlos has been shot. They've carried him up to my room, and Dru's gone for the doctor."

Hannah, without saying another word, climbed the ladder into the wagon. She sat herself down on the mattress and slid an arm across Rosa's shoulders like it was something she did every day.

Hannah

I'D BEEN IN MY ROOM, STARING AT A BLANK PIECE OF PAPER, when the commotion of a team and wagon racing up the drive drew me to the window in the room across the hall. It was the Tinka wagon. Sensing trouble in their speed, I hurried down the stairs. In the resting room, a knot of women had gathered at the open doorway, another at each of the windows. One woman turned to me as I passed. "Why have those people come here?" she asked, a dash of bitters in her tone.

All the lessons about not talking back to my elders flew out the window, and I answered, "They, too, are Eliza's friends."

In the stable, Isaac, bare-chested and grim-faced, stood at the rear of the Tinka wagon. He told me the little he knew before I climbed inside. The mattress Rosa sat on was badly stained, but I took no mind of that. Rosa choked out foreign words I couldn't understand, though I knew what they meant. However the accident had happened, Rosa blamed herself.

"Your brother will be fine," I said again and again and in rhythm with her rocking.

When I thought Rosa was ready, I said, "Go to him. He needs you." And she did. Isaac, who hadn't left his vigil at the rear of the wagon, helped Rosa down and then, taking her elbow, escorted her up the steps.

In the time it took for Isaac to return, I had, by turns, shoved and tugged the mattress out of the wagon and onto the stable floor. "I must wash the stain from this," I said in answer to the question in Isaac's eyes.

"Nobody expects you to."

"Nobody but me. I must do something, and this is the only thing I know to do. The Tinkas shouldn't have to look at this again, especially if Carlos does not . . ."

"I'll fetch water," Isaac said.

I looked around, thinking I'd use a burlap sack for a scrub rag, and there on the floor was a heap of brown cloth. I held the fabric between my teeth and ripped away one strip and then another. When Isaac returned with the bucketful of water, I asked him to pour it on the center of the stain. The stain spread like ink spilled on a blotter. I dropped to my knees and began scrubbing. I scrubbed and scrubbed, using all the strength in my shoulders and arms. Scrubbed and scrubbed, calling for Isaac to bring more water. Scrubbed and scrubbed until the cornhusk stuffing was little more than mush. Scrubbed until I'd worn holes in the ticking. And still I scrubbed, the cobblestones cutting into my knees. Scrubbed and scrubbed until Isaac took hold of my arms and pulled me to my feet.

"It's no good," he said, turning me around. "Let go of it, Hannah."

"I can't let go, not ever," I shrieked. "My brothers are dead. I should have fought harder to get back to the school."

Isaac threw his arms around me then, pulling me tight against his bare chest. I felt safe there, like coming home to a warm house.

Isaac pressed his cheek against mine. "Stop blaming yourself. You did fight hard, Hannah. You fought hard for me, pulling me along even when I'd all but given up. You saved my life, Hannah, though I wasn't worth the saving."

I was about to scold him for saying such an awful thing when we again heard hoof beats on the drive. Isaac unwrapped his arms from about me, backed toward the door leading to the print shop, grinned, and then ducked inside.

"Where's the boy?" a man's voice asked. I spun around. Doctor Forbes was familiar to me. He'd been called to our soddie to treat my and Papa's frostbite in the days after the blizzard. But the man standing next to Dru was young and kindly faced, not elderly and gruff.

"Up there," I said, pointing, and the doctor took the steps two at a time.

Dru stepped around the ruined mattress and asked, "What happened? You look like you've been wrung through the wringer of Eliza's washing machine. And your hands. They're bleeding."

"It's a long story."

"And it's a story you're going to tell me, once you've gotten out of those soiled clothes and we've taken care of your hands."

———————

Later, after I'd changed behind the three-paneled dressing screen in my room, Dru insisted that she dab salve on my scrapes and cuts. Our feet dangling over the edge of the bed, Dru said, "Now you must tell me the story of what happened in the stable. I can't wait a minute longer."

"There's a girl. Her name is Rosa, the sister of the boy who was shot. She's blaming herself, and my heart just broke for her."

"As you are blaming yourself for the loss of your own brothers?"

If it had been an ordinary day, I might have tried to change the subject or made up a reason for excusing myself, but it hadn't been an ordinary day. Like the Tinka mattress, my will had worn to mush. "How much has Isaac told you?"

"Most all, but please don't be angry with him. You know how I am. I hounded him mercilessly."

"Then you know that I wasn't with my brothers as I should have been, know that I shamed myself by spending the night in a haystack with Isaac."

"Nonsense," Dru said, setting the jar of salve aside. "If there is any shame to be handed out, it belongs to those of us who whined that the streets might not be cleared in time for the next evening's entertainment at the opera house. And your father, might not the blame fall squarely on his shoulders? I've heard tell that many a father fetched their children safely home with horse and sleigh."

"He thought we were safe at the school, had no way of knowing the roof had collapsed. And he did go out when he saw that the storm wasn't letting up, but he had to turn back. His feet were nearly as frostbitten as mine."

"But you didn't give up, did you, Hannah? You went on, pulling Isaac along behind you. You're the one who found shelter in the haystack. You're the one who saved another's life."

"Isaac exaggerates. I didn't find the haystack; the wind blew me to it. Isaac's the hero, not me. He kept me warm, and I owe him my life."

"Are you sure you know your own heart, Hannah? Are you sure you feel only friendship for Isaac, like you always say?"

I looked down at my hands as if they could tell me how to answer, tell me how to trust, then raised my eyes to Dru's. "You're right, Dru. I do care for Isaac in a way that's more than friendship, but he deserves a girl who is free to care for him in return, and that's never going to happen. My papa will never approve."

"Your papa and my mother! If she even suspected that I was interested in a country boy, not Isaac, of course, but another country boy, she'd have me packed and on a train headed east to one of those finishing schools she is forever threatening me with, quicker than you can say purple periwinkle."

"Purple periwinkle?"

"It was the first thing that came to mind. But tell me, what might your papa think if you brought Rusty Farley home for Sunday dinner?"

"Dru!"

"Okay, I'll button my lip." And she did button it, for about five seconds. "Oh, did you get a look at the new doctor, the one who just last week hung out his shingle here in town? His office is three blocks closer than the one of old Doc Forbes, so I asked him to come instead. He's so handsome, and young, near the same age as Eliza. Do you suppose he and Eliza might hit it off?"

"Dru, you've been reading too many novels."

Eliza came in my room just then, carrying an armload of Isaac's things. "Good news. Doctor Goodman believes Carlos, if his wound is kept clean and he's given at least a month's rest, will recover. With the Tinkas in the room above the stable, Isaac will have to bunk in one of the empty rooms up here. You don't mind, do you, Hannah?"

"Wouldn't the Tinkas be more comfortable up here,

with beds enough to go around? I . . . I could sleep on the cot in the resting room."

"Their ways are different from ours. That's why I didn't have them bring Carlos up here when they first arrived. In the stable they'll have their privacy, and their wagon home will be close by."

Then Eliza turned to Dru. "I can't thank you enough, Dru, for fetching Doctor Goodman. He used the most modern of medical methods and was a model of efficiency."

"And handsome?" Dru asked.

"Is he? I didn't notice."

I tugged Dru into the hall.

"And a bachelor, quite eligible," Dru said over her shoulder.

I jabbed my elbow into her ribs and, like schoolgirls, we broke out in giggles. Dru, who could turn around the most horrid of days. Dru, who could turn despair into giggles. Dru, my bosom friend.

———

I began work on the play later that evening. Not writing it, just jotting words and phrases on my paper. I propped myself against the headboard of my bed, stuffed a pillow at the small of my back, and drained my mind, which wasn't hard — the happenings of the day had made me like a leaky bucket. One word that didn't drain was "wind" so I wrote it down, and the second was "evil." Evil wind? *Yes*, I thought, the blizzard wind had been evil. Then, through the wall separating Isaac's room from mine, came a quiet cough, and I wrote "good wind." Good and evil — could the wind be both? Thinking to save that question for another time when I wasn't worn so thin, I wrote "school," which led to "teacher," which led to "students," which led to "recess," which led to "Fox and Geese," which led to "crafty like a fox," which led back to "wind." Evil wind, crafty wind, good wind?

It went on like that, one word leading to another. Some word strings even made me laugh, like "snow — drift — shoes — wet socks — Isaac." Others caused shivers, like "haystack — hide — safety — secret — shame." Sometimes the appearance of a word at the end of my pencil jolted me. "Anger" was one of these words. And sometimes I crossed out a word as soon as I'd written it, like "Papa." When I finally laid my pencil aside, leaned back, and squinted, the paper looked like tracks a confused and dizzy chicken had traced across snow. It wasn't much, but it was a beginning, like collecting ingredients for a cake or setting type for the gazette and skipping nine letters out of every ten. In the weeks to come, I'd stir those words up, fill in the empty spaces.

PART III

Late August, 1888

Isaac

I'D BEEN LIVING HIGH ON THE HOG, SLEEPING IN A SLEIGH BED.
Built of the finest mahogany, the bed's headboard and foot-
board topped off in a curlicue. Eliza had offered the bed to
Hannah when she'd first come to live in the house. Hannah
had picked a different room, and I knew why. For Hannah
the sleigh bed had been too hard a reminder of the blizzard.
But I'd managed just fine. August had been sweltering hot,
so thoughts of snow were almost welcome.

Hannah's room was next to mine. The heads of our beds
shared the same wall, so our pillows were only a lathe and
plaster width apart. Sometimes at night I'd be lying there,
trying to catch Hannah's thoughts. I don't know if I ever
did catch a real thought, but I did have some mighty sweet
dreams.

The Tinkas were still on board, and Carlos was on the
mend. They weren't overly talkative types, so the story of
how Carlos had been shot dribbled out only in bits and
pieces. Pasted together, the pieces added up to this: The
Tinkas had camped for the night on the banks of Lincoln
Creek, three miles to the north of Prairie Hill. In the morning, Mr. Tinka had gone off to hunt jackrabbits. Mrs.
Tinka, having asked Rosa to keep an eye on the young ones,
was doing up the wash down by the creek. Rosa was sitting
near the morning fire, braiding her sister's hair, when a shot

rang out from inside the wagon. When Carlos recovered enough to tell his side of the story, he said that he'd been mad at his pa for not asking him to tag along on the hunt and had taken the key to his pa's pistol case from its hiding place. He hadn't remembered much after that, only that he'd been turning the gun over and over in his hands.

Rosa blamed herself, but not for long. Her pa helped her see that it wasn't her fault. I'd been there in the stable that night. I couldn't make out a one of Mr. Tinka's foreign words, but his meaning was spelled out as if in bolded printer's type. He stood in front of Rosa, his finger jabbing at his own chest, not hers. Rosa's eyes were as wide as tomorrow. When Mr. Tinka was done jabbing, he threw his arms around Rosa and held her for longer than I stayed to watch. One man ought not have another fellow watch him cry. Hannah, who'd been standing beside me, didn't budge. It was like she was frozen there.

Some fewer visitors had come to the resting room after the Tinkas set up housekeeping in the stable, one member of the Advisory Council among them, a Mrs. Hadley. After hearing the news, which spread about as fast as a prairie wildfire, she'd shown herself one last time. The way Eliza told it, Mrs. Hadley, nostrils flaring, had demanded, "Those dirty people must be asked to leave at once." Eliza didn't argue, only walked over to the list of "courtesies" that was posted on the wall and pointed to the first — "Every woman, regardless of family circumstance, nationality, or creed, will be welcomed and shown the highest and equal regard."

The Tinkas were anything but dirty. They took great pains when washing up their dishes and clothes. Spoons and plates, one for each Tinka, weren't washed together in the same tub of water, but separately. They did the same thing when they washed their clothes. Where my ma had always divided her wash by color — whites first, in the hottest and cleanest of water — the Tinka women divided their wash by who wore it or what it was used for. Mr. Tinka's drawers never went into the same wash water as his wife's under-things — the tea towels never into the same water as the drawers. And, instead of pegging one wet thing to the other like a mouthful of good teeth, the Tinka women left big gaps on the line when they hung their wash out to dry, which made it look like some of the teeth had fallen out.

Mrs. Hadley hadn't been the only one to hurl rocks at the Tinkas' character. The Reverend Cobb had paid Eliza one of his not-so-social calls. Eliza and I were in the print shop, printing up the latest edition of the gazette when Dru came in saying that the Reverend Cobb wanted a word with Eliza. Eliza rolled her eyes, wiped her inky hands on her apron, and marched out.

I carried a chair to the door, stood on it, and peeked through the transom Mr. Tinka had helped me build into the wall above the door. This transom didn't have frosted window glass like the transoms above all the doors in the main house. Instead it was inset with finely woven black netting that allowed me to see out without easily being seen. The transom was to be my window on the working girls' play, but I'd begun to use it as my window on the world.

The Reverend Cobb tugged at his white-banded collar like it was choking his words. He kept his voice low, likely so as not to be heard by the women in the resting room or, when I lip-read the word "heathens," by God himself. Eliza, chewing her bottom lip, held her tongue until the reverend ran out of word-rocks to throw. Then she let go of her lip and let loose a rock of her own: "And you preach of Christian charity." She nearly knocked me off my chair in her rush to get back into the print shop.

The Reverend Cobb's wife showed up not an hour after the Reverend left. Again Eliza rolled her eyes. Again I climbed on my chair and spied. But there wasn't anything to hear, nothing to see, except for Mrs. Cobb leaning into Eliza's ear and Eliza shaking her head.

Eliza was still shaking her head when she returned to the print shop. "What did she want?" I asked.

"Mrs. Cobb wrongly assumed that Mrs. Tinka was a fortuneteller, wanted her future read, though I wasn't to breathe a word of it to the reverend. So I asked her, 'Does every blind person carry a tin cup?'"

"And?"

"She didn't make the connection. Narrow thinking, that's what's wrong with the world today. Lumping people together like so many stamped-tin soldiers. That's ridiculous. No two of us are exactly alike, no matter what language we speak, what clothes we wear, where we lay our heads down to sleep at night."

I said "amen" to that.

Mrs. Tinka might not have been a fortuneteller, but she had another knack that drew the town women to the resting room. Mrs. Tinka concocted the best tasting bread. So good tasting that I'd once eaten half a loaf at a sitting. No one but the Tinka women knew what went into that bread — a secret family recipe. The crust was crispy, and the center was soft. Hannah thought there might be a touch of dill, Eliza guessed garlic, and my ma was sure she detected molasses. Mrs. Tinka started out baking five loaves for market days, then ten, then twenty, using both her oven and the one in Eliza's kitchen, and still there were women who went away empty-handed. Eliza finally had to set a limit, one loaf per customer, to keep the women from squabbling about who'd been first in line. Mrs. Tinka used the bread money to pay down the debt owed to Doc Goodman.

Mr. Tinka, like me, dared not set foot off Eliza's property. Sheriff Tulley had been the third person to pester Eliza about the Tinkas. I didn't spy through the transom that day, didn't dare move, so I heard the story secondhand from Eliza, which was more and more the case. Life outside the print shop was becoming like a storybook — a book with many of the pages ripped out. Pages about me!

What Eliza told me of the sheriff's visit was this — allowing that the Tinkas were guests of Eliza's and hadn't yet committed a crime, he'd look the other way until Carlos was well enough to travel, so long as Mr. Tinka stayed put. "I've heard tell that those people will stoop so low as to steal the last penny from a blind man's tin cup," the sheriff had said.

"*Some* of their kind, perhaps," Eliza had replied. "As would some of *our* kind, but not the Tinkas. My late husband held Mr. Tinka in the highest regard, said he was a man of honor, a man to be admired for standing tall in the face of ignorant slurs against his character."

I steered clear of Mr. Tinka those first couple of days. I was still hiding out, after all, and he'd caught me wearing a dress. And I wasn't surprised when he came to me, his face as serious as Sunday and only inches away from my own, saying that he'd string me up if I so much as looked crosswise at Rosa. Those were almost the same words Hannah's pa had spat at me the morning after the blizzard. At the rate I was going, I'd be a bachelor the rest of my life.

I told Mr. Tinka that he didn't have a thing to worry about, that I was saving all my sweet talk for another girl.

After that he befriended me, and I was mighty grateful. It'd been months since I'd so much as talked to another fellow. Evenings, after the Tinkas had eaten their supper and we'd eaten ours, he'd lend a hand to the finishing work on my boat. While we worked, he taught me a few of his foreign words. The Tinkas were "rom"; Eliza, Hannah, and I were "gajo." "Dae" was mother. "Posta" was sacrifice.

There was another thing Mr. Tinka did that earned my thanks. To, as he put it, "scratch the moving-on itch," he mowed the grass, pruned the shrubs, and chopped the wood. The next time Rusty Farley showed up there was nothing for him to do but sit on the wagon seat the whole two hours his ma was in the resting room. Eliza invited him inside, but Rusty would have none of it. My regard for Rusty raised a notch when I heard that. No self-respecting boy his age, given a choice, would have set foot inside the resting room, broiling sun or not.

Like me, Hannah was-but-wasn't there during those weeks of late July and early August. She did her share of the work — dusted and scrubbed, collected the monies on market days, and set type for the gazette — but she wasn't there in her thoughts. Her thoughts were tied up in the crumpled papers she carried and in the stubby pencil she wore above her ear. Whenever she found herself with a minute to spare, she wrote. And even when she wasn't writing on her paper, she was writing in her head. I'd catch her staring blank-eyed at a wall or drifting away between fork-fuls of her supper.

Hannah wouldn't tell me or anyone else for that matter what the play was about, but if one paid attention — and when it came to Hannah I always paid attention — you could figure it out. My first clue came one evening. She'd left her bedroom door ajar, and I just happened to glance in as I passed by. She was standing at the window and had twisted herself up in the long, lacy curtain. The curtain's crocheted pattern was the giveaway; the weave looked like a swirl of snowflakes.

Another evening, it being my turn for kitchen duty, I was up to my elbows in dishwater when I heard Hannah humming a happy tune out in the main hall. I peeked, and there was Hannah, dancing with the dust mop. Not dancing free like she'd danced across the prairie, but swaying enough to stir her skirts. I wished later that I hadn't peeked, because when Hannah caught me grinning at her, she got that star-tled look of a fox caught in the hen house, stopped her dancing, and went back to hunting dust furries with her mop.

Then there was the night of the storm. I'd been in the stable, working on my boat, when a gust of wind, the smell of rain on its breath, slammed the stable doors shut. When I opened the doors again, lightning forked white-hot against the black sky. I went looking for Hannah, upstairs and down, all the while the thunderclaps rattled the windows like cold chatters teeth. I was checking the parlor for a second time when a lightning flash lit the window to the veranda. There was Hannah. Bracing herself with her hands, she leaned out over the rail. I lost her to darkness, then another flash lit her again. The way she stood there so still, she might have been one of those carved lady figureheads that decorated the prows of the old-time ships I'd seen pictured in one of the Judge's boat-building books.

I joined Hannah then, leaned out over the rail and tried to feel what she felt. Tried to imagine what she was imagining. All I felt was rain splatting against my face. All I imagined was Mr. Richards hollering at me, saying that I didn't have a brain enough to know when to come in out of the rain.

After a bit Hannah turned to me and said, "I have a favor to ask."

"Name it."

"Teach me how to spit."

If I hadn't been holding the rail, I might have fallen overboard. "Girls don't . . ." I started to say.

"You'd better not let Eliza hear you talk like that."

So I taught Hannah to spit, with the wind first, then into the wind, right there on the veranda, right there in the middle of that thunderstorm.

Hannah

JUST BEFORE DAWN ON A RAINY AUGUST MORNING, THE FLICKER of lamplight shadow-dancing across my papers, I leaned back against my pillow and laid my pencil aside. The play I'd wanted to write, needed to write, was finished. Done.

I slipped out of bed, then padded down the stairs, careful not to disturb the sleepers. I crept past the portrait of Madeline Moore with her wise, watchful eyes. Past the hush of the fern-filled parlor, the Judge's library with its wall of books, into and through Eliza's kitchen and laundry. On reaching the resting room, I built a fire in the potbelly stove then settled into one of the rocking chairs, cradling the play in my lap. Using the fire for light, I reread the first page, with its narrator telling of children setting off for school, ankle-deep in fresh fallen snow, then, like the curtain opening, I fed the page to the fire. The edges curled, caught, burst into flames. I held my hands over the rising heat, warming them.

Into the flames, page by page, like curtains opening and closing, the scenes played out. Page after page until there were no pages left in my lap.

Ash and smoke — the only possible end. I'd written *my* story, not the working girls' story, not the story of the people who would attend the play. No one had been spared the blizzard's fury, be they trapped outside or in. I think before I'd finished writing the first page I knew the play would never, could never, be performed, but once I'd begun, buried myself waist-deep in its drifts, there was no turning back.

I told no one that I'd burned the first play, not even Isaac. It wouldn't have done for Isaac to know the whole of it because I'd written everything I remembered. About how close Isaac had held me and how warm he had made me feel. About not wanting to die. And the next morning wishing that I had.

When anyone asked, and Dru asked every day, how the play was coming along, I smiled and said, "Nicely." This was a stretch but not a lie. Minutes after feeding the first play to the fire, I returned to my room, took up a fresh sheet of paper, and began writing the play the working girls would perform. A play that would belong to all.

I finished the second play in little more than a week. The following Wednesday evening, the working girls pulled their chairs into the usual circle, and I handed out the typeset scripts. Then, after briefly summarizing the scenes and cast of characters, I asked for a show of hands of those interested in the two roles that would require more memorization and extra time for practice. Dru, who had been sitting on the very edge of her chair, raised her hand so fast she was soon sitting on the floor.

"Anyone else?" I asked. I looked around the circle for volunteers. As if suddenly distracted by a piece of lint on their skirts or a creepy-crawly on the ceiling, no eyes met mine and no hands shot up, which would have been particularly hard for Imogene and Gertrude, because they were sitting on theirs. Then Clarice bent a wrist and raised a finger.

Dru, still sitting on the floor, arm still raised, looked up to Clarice. "Would you mind terribly if I took the villainous role?"

Clarice's grin said it all.

The remaining roles were decided by drawing slips of paper from one of Eliza's many hats, save for one. Rosa, with her parents' permission, had agreed to dance in one of the later scenes. I drew the role of the narrator, which suited me just fine.

We went through the play that first night, sitting in our chairs, each girl reading her assigned lines from the script. There was a lot of giggling — from everyone but Dru. Dru was stone-faced serious and slipped into her character as if into a pair of perfectly fitting though sharply pointed shoes.

Every Wednesday evening after that was given over to rehearsals. Each rehearsal brought changes to the script, until, when I finally got it right, there were as many handwritten lines as there were typeset ones. And each rehearsal brought changes in Dru. It was as if once in character the real Dru disappeared — poof! She'd snap at the other girls when they missed a line or exited left instead of right, and she was especially hard on Clarice, the one girl least likely to complain. It got so bad on one particular evening that I walked up to Dru, pretended to rap on her forehead as if it were a door, and asked, "Dru, are you in there?"

Dru stiffened, but just as quickly relaxed. "I'm sorry, Hannah. I've been awful, haven't I? I just want everything to be perfect, but I promise I'll be good from here on out."

She wasn't as snappish with the other girls after that, though her eyes got a lot of exercise from rolling about.

Two weeks before the play was to begin, the handbills had been printed, posted at Fowler's, and sent home with every woman, town or farm, who had visited the resting room or shopped at our market. The costumes, stitched together by some of the regular visitors to the resting room, were nearing readiness.

One week before the play was to begin, the stage had been set. The raised floor in the resting room, from which the Judge had once passed down his verdicts, worked perfectly. When the girls weren't on stage, they could slip into the laundry or indoor necessary to change costumes or wait for their next cue without being seen by the audience.

We'd taken down the heavy velvet draperies that hung at

the wide windows in Eliza's parlor and strung them on a taut rope above the front edge of the stage. Mr. Tinka and Isaac had threaded and looped the rope about a series of pulleys, allowing the curtains to be opened or closed, half to one side and half to the other. Bed sheets, wires threaded through the hems, hung at either side and across the back. At stage left the sheets draped around a paneless window that hung, and sometimes swayed, from wires attached to the ceiling; at stage right, a door was mounted in a footed frame Isaac had ingeniously designed and hammered together.

The Sunday afternoon before the play was to begin, I slipped out to the barn where Papa was tending to Hap's injured hoof. I knelt in the straw near him, drew in a deep breath, and then said, "I'd like it if you could come to Eliza's on Wednesday evening, to see our play."

Papa didn't turn to me.

"I wrote the play, Papa, and I'd like for you to be there."

Still nothing.

"The play is about the blizzard. It's about how hard it was on everyone."

Papa stopped salving. His spine stiffened. "It's not right to make light of folks dying."

"The play isn't like that, Papa. I've tried hard to honor those who lost their lives, but it's also about those who survived, about life going on. You'll see for yourself if you come."

He reached up and patted Hap's haunch. "Hay will be ready to cut come Wednesday. Likely be in the fields until dark."

I got up off my knees then, brushed away the straw clinging to my skirts, and said, "Guess I'd better be heading back."

I was almost to the barn door when Papa called out, "Tell James I said he should hitch up Hazard and drive you back to town. Sun's setting earlier now, and a girl oughtn't be walking the roads after dark."

It took me a moment to steady myself.

———————

Two evenings before the play was to begin, Isaac's mother walked into the resting room. She carried a well-worn leather valise that was nearly the color of the angry bruise on her cheek. I hurried her into the print shop, where Isaac and Eliza were finishing up the play programs. Isaac, on seeing the bruise, became a bull in a cramped corral. He paced back and forth, repeatedly ramming one fisted hand into the palm of the other and saying, "I'll bust his jaw."

"Busting a jaw never solved anything," Eliza said.

"Then I'll bust his gut."

Tears welled in Mrs. Richards's eyes. "If you go after

him, then he's won — turned my sweet boy into a mean cuss of a man."

Isaac stopped his pacing, stopped his fist-slamming, and his face went soft as he slid an arm across his mother's shoulders. "Don't cry, Ma. I'm not like him. I'll never be like him. I promise I won't, but you've got to promise me that you'll not go back, that you'll stay here, where I can keep you safe."

Mrs. Richards sniffed and nodded.

Isaac looked to Eliza then. "That'd be okay, wouldn't it, if my ma stayed here with me?"

"Of course."

"You're so kind," Mrs. Richards said, "but I'll not stay unless I can pay my own way. I've heard tell that women here in Prairie Hill pay good money to have someone come to their homes and do their ironing."

Isaac and I shared a glance and a thought. Isaac's mother had forgotten one thing. If she was seen about town, eventually Mr. Richards would find out.

"You can worry about that in a couple of days, Ma, after your bruise loses its color. Until then, until Mr. Richards cools off, you'd best lie low."

And so Mrs. Richards went into hiding with Isaac.

———

The evening before the play was to begin, Dru and I were carrying the last of the chairs in from the main house. Dru set her chair down at the end of a row, then said, "We've had a telegram from Mother. Auntie's health is much improved, so Mother is returning home, which means that I'll have to sneak here on the sly."

"When do you expect her?"

"We can't be sure. The telegram ended in the middle of one of Mother's long-winded sentences. Whatever day it is, it will be too soon."

"A whole summer too late, from what I hear," Mrs. Callahan's voice boomed. It took only four strides for her to cross from the door to where Dru and I were standing. "I arrive home from an exhausting journey, and the only one there to greet me is the hired help."

"Her name is Clarice, Mother."

"Don't take that tone with me, young lady. Sniveling girl wouldn't tell me a thing. Had to find out where you were and what you've been up to from the Reverend Cobb's wife. Working here like common trash, socializing with my friends' hired girls, and mixing with vulgar foreigners. You've shamed me, Dru. I'll not be able to hold my head up in this town ever again."

I took a step back from the heat in Mrs. Callahan's voice. Dru caught up one of my hands and laced her fingers in mine.

"It's not only farm women who come here, Mother, but women from the town as well. Why, I don't believe there is one among your friends who has not visited the market, Mrs. Cobb included."

Mrs. Callahan's hand slapped over her heart. "I go away for but a few months, and the whole town backslides in my absence. This is Eliza Moore's doing. She's filled your head, corrupted the better women in this town, with her blasphemous political tripe. I'll put a stop to this place before the week is out."

Mrs. Callahan took hold of Dru's arm and yanked her toward the door. Dru's grip on my hand was so strong that I was pulled along with them like we were three children in a game of Crack the Whip.

"Did I hear my name?" Eliza said, rushing in from the print shop.

"Indeed you did," Mrs. Callahan hissed. "But don't worry, I'll speak it no more, nor will my daughter."

"Why don't you come with me to the parlor, where we can discuss this in private, as one sensible woman to another."

"This is not a social call. I am here to remove my daughter from your grasp. You are nothing more than a thief, robbing other mothers' cradles to fill your empty one. And I know about you, met a society woman from Boston in the Pullman car of the train. She told me you were a street beggar when the Judge's mother took you in. And she wasn't in her grave a month when you weaseled your way into her son's affections."

Isaac, who had been down in the cellar feeding coal to the boiler, walked into the resting room just then. His face was dusted with soot, making his startled eyes appear twice their size.

Dru leaned into my ear, whispered, "I'll be back, I promise," then released my hand. "Let's go, Mother," she said, then took up her mother's elbow and guided her toward the door.

"Dru, tell me you've not been consorting with that wild-eyed boy. Tell me it isn't so."

"Of course not, Mother. He's nothing but Eliza's stable boy." And then they were gone.

"Are we in trouble?" Isaac asked.

"Could be," Eliza answered. "When Mrs. Callahan gets riled, there's no telling what she might do."

I turned to Eliza. "Those things she said to you were so cruel and untrue."

"She meant to hurt, yes, but much of what she said is true. Harlan's mother did take me in. She sent me to the finest schools, treated me like a daughter."

"That gives her no right to call you a beggar."

"That part is true, as well. I was a beggar, going around to the back doors of the wealthy, begging my supper. When you are hungry, you do what you must do. I wasn't much younger than you, Hannah, the day Harlan's mother opened her door and pulled me in from the pouring rain. Within the hour, she'd filled my empty belly and opened her heart and home to me. Harlan was older, away at college those first years. It wasn't until I'd grown to be a young woman that he took an interest in me and I in him. Oh, how the society tongues did scandal-wag. They were so vicious, Harlan decided to move his law practice west. We chose Prairie Hill because it sounded like such a pleasant place."

The pieces fitted together like squares in a quilt. Eliza's being so different from the other wealthy women in town. Wanting to change the laws so other girls didn't have to slave in sweatshops or beg their suppers. Her taking me in when she'd already hired Isaac.

Later that evening, badly in need of a few moments of calm, I asked Isaac if he would mind going for a short stroll with me. "I don't know," he said, rubbing his chin. "Are you sure you want to consort with a stable boy?"

"Only with the most handsome of stable boys," I answered.

Isaac grinned and slipped his hand into mine.

Outside, the Tinkas were sitting around their campfire, even Carlos, who was fast regaining his health. Romantic music flowed from Mr. Tinka's fiddle strings. Isaac and I, still holding hands, stood behind them for a time. *How lucky the Tinkas are,* I thought. Mother, father, children, all together, not broken apart like my family, like Isaac's and Eliza's families. I felt the old sadness settling in. *Not tonight,* I scolded myself, then tugged Isaac toward the rear of Eliza's property.

The prairie beyond was as dark as the sky. One wouldn't have known it was there except for the wind threading a whisper through the grasses and its dew-dampened scent. I might have been caught up in a moment of forgetfulness, if Isaac hadn't beat me to it. He let go of my hand, reached into his hip pocket, pulled out his harmonica, and began to play a lovely and vaguely familiar tune of his own. I did not try to stop him.

"Hannah music," he said when he'd finished.

"Hannah music?"

"I used to watch you, when you were out on the prairie, and I made up harmonica tunes to match the way you moved."

And then I remembered. The faint music I'd sometimes heard, that I'd thought had come from inside my head, had been made by Isaac all along. A shiver, warm not cold, passed through me. It was that same shiver I'd once thought shameful. But I felt no shame that night, only joy.

I was about to ask Isaac to play another of his Hannah tunes when there came a shout of "Who goes there?" from the direction of the Tinka campfire. Turning, I saw that Mr. Tinka was on his feet, heading toward the stable. Isaac stuffed his harmonica back into his pocket, took up my hand, and held it extra tight.

We stood there in the dark, waited and listened until Mr. Tinka, shrugging his shoulders, returned to the fire.

"We should go inside," I said.

Isaac sighed. "I suppose we should."

I was tending the market late that next morning, when Clarice rushed in. Her face was damp with perspiration. "Mrs. Callahan has me running all over town," she said when she'd caught her breath. "Telling the women of the Betterment Society of an emergency meeting at the Callahan house."

"Dru?" I asked.

"Mrs. Callahan's mighty mad, has forbidden Dru from ever coming to the resting room again, but before I left, Dru told me to tell you that she promises to be here even if she has to sneak out her window. It's Carol that can't make it."

"Oh, I hope Carol's not ill?"

"No, but her mother is, and Carol has gone along home to help out. Whatever shall we do?"

"I'll think of something."

Having more stops to make, Clarice soon excused herself. What to do? Carol's character wouldn't make an appearance until late in the play, though it was an important role, with more than a few lines. I couldn't ask one of the other girls — there wasn't time. Eliza? No, she had more than enough work behind the scenes to keep her busy, frazzled busy. After whittling down the choices, I was left with only one. I would have to take on both Carol's role and my own.

Thirty minutes before the play was to begin, all the girls except Dru were backstage. I didn't panic, but if I'd been wearing an apron my hands would have been knotted in it.

Fifteen minutes before the play was to begin, my family arrived. I watched the door as they filed in — Mama, Hester, Lila, Megan, Jake, James, and Joey.

Jake and James found leaning room against a wall where a group of boys and young men already leaned, Mary's fiancé and Rusty Farley among them.

Joey tugged my skirts. "Mama says me and Megan gets to see a puppet show."

"That's right, a puppet show just for children. No grownups allowed."

"Oh, boy."

I motioned to Cass, whose sisters had agreed to entertain the youngest children, and she led Megan and Joey behind the curtains. From there they would be climbing the stairs to the nursery on the second floor, which Eliza had so generously offered.

"I'd like to sit in the back if you can find me a place," Mama said.

Like church, the chairs in the back were filled, though no one was sitting on the velvet settee, so I directed Mama there. When she and Hester and Lila were seated, I asked, "Did Papa bring you?"

"He's here, but I couldn't persuade him to come inside. Said he'll wait for us in the wagon."

If I hadn't been so disappointed, I might have been amused by this shift in the wind. Always before it had been one of us waiting for Papa in the wagon.

———————

Five minutes before the play was to begin, Dru made good on her promise. I wanted to take her aside, say something comforting, but when I approached her, she waved me off, saying she needed to be alone, to get into character.

———————

Thirty seconds before the play was to begin, I stepped through the part in the curtain and stationed myself at the left side of the stage.

———————

Five breaths before the play was to begin, I nodded to Flossy and Mrs. Farley, the signal that they were to dim the room's gaslights.

Three breaths before the play was to begin, I nodded to Mr. Tinka, who was seated in the front row with his family. He tucked his fiddle under his chin and raised his bow.

———————

Two breaths before the play was to begin, feeling a hiccup coming on, I pictured a coffin.

———————

One very deep breath before the play began, I looked to the transom. I nodded and smiled.

Isaac

WHEN HANNAH SENT ME THAT LAST LOOK, MY HEART DID A somersault. Ma, standing on a chair beside me, must have seen the look, too. She reached over and patted my arm. Mr. Tinka fiddled a breezy mood, and Hannah, looking as pretty as I'd ever seen her, began the narration.

"Long ago, in the far away, flat as a flapjack, prairie land, there lived The Sisters Wind. One sister, Fair Wind, was kindly and shy, while the other, named Wild Wind, was brash and quarrelsome.

"There were in the same land peasants living in thatched cottages. Of the two sisters, the peasants loved only Fair Wind, for she sang a peaceful song. Never had she torn thatch from their cottage roofs nor broken the limbs from their precious few trees nor sent them chasing after their bonnets and caps, all the things Wild Wind was fond of doing. At the very least, Wild Wind was considered by the peasants to be a bother. At her worst, and winter was the season when Wild Wind was her most wicked, she was considered an abomination.

"When time began, the Sisters Wind shared the throne, taking turns performing their appointed tasks. Wild Wind scattered seeds from one corner of the land to the other, dried the mushy spring soil, and hurried migrating geese, north or south, depending on the season. Fair Wind provided the breeze, cooling the peasants' brows in summer's heat, giving glide to butterflies. As time passed, however, Wild Wind grew more and more jealous of the peasants' love for Fair Wind, until her jealousy soured to bitterness and greed. Of late, she has taken to locking Fair Wind away in the castle's dungeon. Only when Wild Wind finds herself in need of a rest does she allow her sister to sit upon the throne.

"Let us go there now — to the throne room of their castle, in the dead of winter."

The pulleys I'd rigged up hummed when Eliza tugged the ropes to open the curtains. In the center of the stage stood the Judge's leather wing chair, which Mr. Tinka and I had hauled in from the main house. Flanking the chair were two back-breaking potted ferns from Eliza's parlor. The working girls, wearing aprons that had been cut and stitched together from rough burlap, were busy at their chores. Cass and Gertrude worked their brooms; Imogene and Mary, their feather dusters. Sadie was lounging on the throne, admiring her fingernails. Inga, playing the role of the castle guard, stepped on stage and hollered, "Enter Wild Wind."

Sadie popped out of the throne like a kernel of corn from a sizzling skillet. Mr. Tinka played a frenzied flurry. The girls, heads bowed, dropped to their knees.

Dru, wearing a long hooded cape made of silky black cloth, stomped into the scene. She stomped a circle around the stage, then plopped herself in the chair not at all gracefully.

"Wild Wind has tuckered herself out," Hannah then said. "All night she has been blowing sickness across the land. In the morning, many of the peasant children will awake with scratchy throats and rattling coughs."

Dru raised a hand to her mouth, as if to stifle a yawn, then hiccupped.

"Oh, my, Wild Wind, in hiccupping, has inhaled the sickness into her own lungs."

Dru sneezed, then, pointing from Imogene to Gertrude to Sadie, she wheezed out a string of demands. "Bring me my slippers, my shawl — get me handkerchiefs and the bottle of Doctor Marvel's Miracle Medicinal Elixir."

The girls trooped off, then returned one by one. When the slippers were on Dru's feet and the shawl draped over her shoulders, Dru trumpeted her nose into one of the handkerchiefs, then pretended to swig the elixir. She wiped her mouth on her sleeve, then hiccupped. She coughed and sneezed, then rammed her hands deep into her pockets. Out came a blizzard of wind-spoiled things — tree twigs and crushed leaves, feathers and robins' egg shells, and a battered peasant's cap (belonging to yours truly). Dru dove in her pockets one more time and dragged out a rattle of keys, which she tossed to Inga. "Bring my sister to me, and be quick about it. And the rest of you, clean up this mess."

Mr. Tinka played busy music while the girls tidied up the floor around the throne.

Hannah stepped forward. All heads, including mine, swiveled in her direction. "The castle guard makes her way down and into the dark, dank dungeon, where Fair Wind is imprisoned. Fair Wind greets the guard with her usual cheery smile. When the guard turns the key in the lock and swings open the barred door, Fair Wind fairly floats up the stairs."

Shortly, Inga showed herself at the side curtain again, marched over to Dru, handed her the keys, and then said, "Enter Fair Wind."

Clarice, wearing the same kind of cape as Dru, only colored sky blue, butterfly-danced into the scene. She flittered a circle around the throne, then knelt before Dru and took up her hand. "The castle guard tells me you are feeling poorly, sister. Shall I help you to your bed?"

Dru made a move to shove Clarice away but was set upon by a coughing spell. When the spell passed, she said, "If I leave you in charge, you can breathe a breeze now and again, but you must promise to do nothing more."

Clarice's back was to the audience, so everyone saw how she reached around and crossed her fingers. "I promise."

After that, Dru made no fuss. Steadying herself on Clarice's arm, she left the scene. The working girls, grinning like it was the last day of school, joined hands and began to skip a circle around the throne. Mr. Tinka's music grinned, too.

When Clarice returned, the girls gathered around her. "Wild Wind has blown sickness into the air," Gertrude said.

"Oh, dear. That will never do." Clarice stepped to the front edge of the stage then and, a hand at her brow like a soldier's salute, she leaned from side to side like she was looking out across the land. She shook her head the way people do when they see a sorry sight, then said back over her shoulder, "I'd be ever so pleased if one of you could fetch my basket of magic snow."

You'd have thought the girls were fetching a pot of gold the way they galloped off stage, elbows flying. When they came back, all had at least one hand on the basket, which made them mighty clumsy, which accounted for some laughs in the audience. Clarice rested the basket on her hip, then tossed scissored bits of paper high in the air. Mr. Tinka plucked the fiddle strings ever so lightly, which was his way of making the music of falling snow. When her basket was half empty, Clarice glided toward the door I'd hung in the footed frame. She waved, stepped through, then closed the door behind her. Eliza closed the curtain.

All eyes on Hannah again, she said, "All night, while Wild Wind snorted and snored in her bed, Fair Wind stayed at her work, turning the sickness Wild Wind had scattered into harmless, crystalline snow. So delighted is she that she doesn't return to the castle until the snow, pretty as velvety icing on a cake, has piled up a foot deep all across the land."

Hannah ducked behind the curtain then, and Mr. Tinka played a screechy note. Off stage Eliza banged pot lids together, three times and thunderously. Also off stage, Dru shouted, "Sister. I take a little nap and you undo all my hard work. Tricked me into thinking I was at death's door so you . . . so you . . . so you could please the sniveling, ungrateful peasants. I'll put a stop to your funny business, as soon as you bring me my shoes."

"But sister, you have gotten up on the wrong side of the bed," Clarice said. "You should not go out when you are so cross."

"I'll go where I want, when I want, thank you very much. Now get me my shoes!"

Behind the curtain there was groaning and moaning, stomping, shuffling, and surly sighing.

When the curtain opened, Dru started in spinning around the stage like a drunken twister. Clarice, head lowered, stood off to one side, and the servant girls, down on their knees, cowered and quaked. Dru spun to a stop, dug in her pocket for the keys, and then tossed them to Inga. "Lock her up, and don't give her any supper."

"Promise me you won't do anything foolish," Clarice pleaded as Inga led her away.

"Promises, shromishes," Dru spat back, then rubbed her

hands together in an fiendish way and slunk toward the door. Before going out, Dru turned and said, "I'll show you who rules this land," then laughed a breathy, evil laugh.

The servant girls rushed to the window. "Oh, my," Cass said, pointing, "see there, see how the air sparks."

"And see how the thermometer plummets," added Gertrude.

Mary wrung her hands. "I've never seen Wild Wind this angry."

Mr. Tinka played then, music that was harsh and rasping and loud. Blizzard music. Inga slipped back on stage.

The girls were still standing at the window, still wringing their hands, when there came a knock at the door. They huddled together like they were trying to decide what to do.

Then came another, louder, door-wobbling knock.

Still the girls huddled.

And then a third knock, loud enough to wake the dead.

The girls shoved Inga toward the door, where she asked, "Friend or foe?"

"I come as a friend. Please, will you give me shelter from the storm?"

"Oh, no, we mustn't. If we break the rules Wild Wind will have our heads," Inga answered.

"Wrong rules are meant to be broken. Perhaps, if I could have a word with Fair Wind?"

"Fair Wind is locked away in the dungeon, and Wild Wind has the key," Sadie hollered.

Inga, looking kind of sheepish, reached into her pocket, and out came the dungeon keys. "Wild Wind left before I could return them," she said. "Do I dare free Fair Wind without her permission?"

The girls huddled again. "Wild Wind will eat us for her supper," one said.

"Or burn us at the stake."

"Maybe, but maybe not. If she was rid of us, who would clean up her messes?"

"Please," came the voice.

"Let's take a vote," Inga said. "All in favor of freeing Fair Wind from the dungeon raise your right hand."

Imogene's hand was the first to shoot up, followed by Mary's, and then, one by one, all hands were raised, and Inga ducked behind the side curtain.

"Fair Wind will be here shortly," Sadie said to the door.

There wasn't an answer.

Cass pressed her ear to the wood. "Maybe she got tired of waiting and left."

Gertrude pretended to chew her fingernails, then said, "Or maybe she froze to death."

Sadie lifted the latch just as Clarice breezed on stage. "Yes, by all means, open the door."

Scissored snow, thrown by Eliza, blew in right along with Hannah.

"It's bad, then?" Clarice asked.

"Yes, very bad. The worst I've ever seen. Wild Wind has blown up a blizzard, and it has hit like a fist. There is no north. No south, east, or west, only Wild Wind. Wild Wind and her foul breath, pummeling the peasants, sucking up the flames from their fires, ripping the roofs from their cottages. If I hadn't seen your light, if you hadn't opened your door to me, I would surely have been lost."

"Can she stay?" Cass asked.

"Yes, of course. She can stay until the storm passes," Clarice answered.

Then came another knock at the door. Clarice opened it, and standing there was none other than Rusty Farley, saying, "I thought I was lost until I saw the light." The working girls giggled into their hands, and then, after smoothing their aprons and plumping their hair, dragged Rusty by his arms and shoved him into the wing chair. He tried to get up, but they shoved him back down, then, leaving Inga behind to guard him, the other girls shot off in all directions. They soon returned, carrying shawls and slippers.

Hannah and Clarice were talking quietly to each other, and the girls were fussing over Rusty, when there came a third knock at the door — Mary's fiancé, saying, "I thought

I was lost until I saw the light." Mary wasted no time tugging him to the far side of the stage. Doc Goodman's was the next knock, followed by Eliza's.

While the girls cocooned the new arrivals in blankets and shawls, Hannah and Clarice took center stage. "Wild Wind has gone too far. Isn't there something you can do?" Hannah asked.

"I'm sorry, but it would take a dozen of me to stop Wild Wind."

Hannah turned, raised an index finger, and counted heads. "If we all made believe, harder than ever before, could we become like you, if only for a little while?"

Clarice scrunched her brow. "Perhaps, but you would need to learn my magic dance."

"Please, will you teach us?"

"I could, but there is one who is a better teacher than I, the one who taught me to dance when I was very young. Shall I call her?"

"Yes, please do," Hannah answered.

Clarice squeezed her eyes shut like she was wishing hard, and Rosa tiptoed onto the stage. Clarice did one of those girlish curtsies, then said, "I'm so glad you've come. Please, might you be willing to teach my friends the dance?"

Rosa looked from one to the other of the folks on stage, like she was sizing them up, then grinned and nodded, and right away the blankets and shawls came off and everyone shuffled themselves into two lines. Hannah hid herself behind the biggest person on stage — Doc Goodman.

"Do as I do," Rosa said.

And that's what they did. When Rosa stepped a foot forward then back — the cast stepped a foot forward and back. When Rosa, one arm raised, dipped at the waist — they raised and they dipped, and so on and so forth until everyone had gotten the hang of the moves Rosa had built into the dance.

This part of the play had been rehearsed only once because it had taken so long to convince the fellows that they wouldn't become the laughing stock of the county. Rusty's dancing was on the clumsy side, but even if I'd been out there leaning against the wall instead of standing on a chair in the dark, I wouldn't have snickered, because I was too busy scowling. The only reason a fellow, any fellow, me included, would have agreed to get up there on that stage, risk making himself out to be a fool, would be to win a girl's heart.

I was still scowling when music as sweet as clover honey started oozing from Mr. Tinka's fiddle. It was mighty hard to hold my scowl after that, and darned near impossible once Rosa started in dancing like she'd done the night I'd been stuck up the tree. She wove in and out, dipped and twirled.

A couple of times Doc Goodman dipped left when he should have dipped right, letting me see more of Hannah than a foot or an arm. The look on her face, the one she always got when she was thinking extra hard, told me Hannah wasn't play-acting. She was making believe that the dance could stop the wind for real.

The dancing went on for a few minutes, and then there came a final knock at the door. Inga glided over, opened it, and then froze — solid as an iced-over cornstalk. Everyone on stage froze in whatever position they'd been in. Mr. Tinka, too, elbow high, cut short in the middle of an upward stroke.

Dru, gasping dramatically, made her grand entrance. Staggering this way and that like she'd drunk too much whisky, she aimed for center stage. Once she got there, which took a while, she put a hand to throat, wheezed, "I can't breathe," and then collapsed to the floor, slow and liquid as a spring thaw.

And then something happened that wasn't in any of the rehearsals I'd spied on. The curtain jerked, jerked, jerked shut. I didn't have an inkling who'd yanked the rope so hard and fast like that. Not Eliza — she was on stage. Everyone in the play was on stage. Whoever it was didn't know squat about pulleys. One more jerk and the whole thing would have come crashing down and Hannah's play would have been sunk.

Whispers then, and footsteps. Folks shifting in their chairs. Voices, garbled but angry, and none too soon drowned out by Mr. Tinka's furious and ear-splitting fiddle.

The curtain opened then, careful like, and the people on the stage started in dancing again. Everyone except Hannah, Dru, and Eliza. They were nowhere in sight.

Hannah

HIDDEN BEHIND DOC GOODMAN AS I WAS, AND CAUGHT UP IN making believe that a dance could truly stop the wind, the curtain was halfway closed before it attracted my attention, though things moved quickly after that. Dru's mother marched on stage, grabbed Dru's arm, yanked her to her feet, and then marched her off. Dru must have been stunned, because she didn't protest or try to pull away. Eliza dashed after them. I leaned close to Rosa's ear and whispered, "Keep dancing."

As I reached for the rope to reopen the curtains, Mr. Tinka, dear Mr. Tinka, without a cue from me, began to play. Loud enough, I hoped, to muffle the quarrel that was brewing in the laundry.

The quarrel had moved outdoors by the time I'd made my way through the laundry and joined Eliza in the darkened kitchen. We listened at the door, which they'd left ajar.

"Please, Mother, I'm the star of the play, and it can't go on without me."

"Being the star in a working girls' play is like being the smartest dunce."

"That's not true. It's a good play. My friend Hannah wrote it."

"And I suppose the next thing you're going to tell me is

that that thieving, harmonica-playing stable boy composed the score."

My stomach knotted.

"What . . . what do mean?" Dru asked.

"I mean I know Eliza Moore has been hiding a criminal here all summer. I paid your father's handyman a dollar to come here last night, and he told me he heard harmonica music. It wasn't until a short time ago that I remembered the sheriff was searching for a boy who played the harmonica. If the sheriff weren't over in the next county on some kind of business, that boy would be locked up by now, Eliza Moore right along with him, and the abomination you call the resting room would be shut down. As for you, young lady, I've already sent a telegram of inquiry to Miss Pritchard's Finishing School in Boston."

For a moment, the only voice I heard was the one screaming in my head. *Convince her that she's wrong, that Isaac isn't a thief, that the resting room does only good. Do it now, Dru, before it's too late. Now, Dru!*

"Please, Mother, if I come with you, promise never to set foot in here again, will you promise not to send me away? Please, I'm begging you." Dru's voice was as small and child-like as Megan's.

I turned and walked toward the sounds of Mr. Tinka's fiddle. Eliza close behind, I passed through the kitchen, the laundry, and onto the stage. On seeing me, Mr. Tinka lowered his bow and Rosa stepped aside. I looked up to the transom and said, "We the peasants of this flat-as-a-flapjack prairie land have no more to fear from Wild Wind tonight. In coming together, joining with Fair Wind in her dance, we have stolen the wind from her sails, silenced her roar."

I turned to the cast then and, skipping ahead two pages in the script, said, "Let the celebration begin."

Relief blossomed on the working girls' faces and from the strings of Mr. Tinka's fiddle. The dancing began — this time in pairs, a rollicking two-step. Mary danced with her fiancé, Clarice, with Doc Goodman (until Eliza cut in), and the working girls each took Rusty for a grinning spin.

Soon, and as planned, the music slowed and hushed — the cue for Clarice to escort the peasant guests, one by one, to the door. She bid each the same farewell. "Go, make your roofs strong, plant many trees, and always keep a candle burning at each of your windows so the lost might find their way home."

I was the last to leave, closing the door behind me. I turned down the wick on the gaslight to the right of the stage, Eliza, the one to the left, and the working girls were thrown into near darkness. Forming a half circle behind Clarice, the girls drew candles from their apron pockets. Clarice struck a match, touched it to her candle's wick, then said, "We dedicate this play to those who did not find shelter from Wild Wind in the blizzard of January twelve, Eighteen Hundred and Eighty Eight. We'd like especially to honor those who were lost here in Prairie County."

The room grew deathly quiet as Clarice lit Inga's candle from her own. Inga stepped forward. "Katie Cathcart, age six, the daughter of Guy and Elizabeth Cathcart, lost at Harmony School."

Inga stepped back, lit Mary's candle, and then Mary stepped forward. "Jon Barnett, age eight, the son of Joseph and Ione Barnett, lost at Harmony School."

And then Sadie. "Jacob Barnett, age ten, the son of Joseph and Ione Barnett, lost at Harmony School."

My brothers' names, spoken clear and loud, was the one selfish thing I carried over from the first play to the second. It was my gift to them, my way of taking them out of hiding. Since the funeral, their names had been spoken only in whispers. Whispers tell secrets, dole out shame. Jon and Jacob had done nothing shameful. They deserved to have their names shouted from the rooftops, not hidden away in some cold, dark, sad place in our thoughts and hearts.

———————

"When next the wind blows strong out of the north, light a candle in remembrance," Clarice said when the last name had been spoken.

Eliza closed the curtain.

One person began to clap, and then another and another until growing into a thunder of applause. I turned the gaslight to full wick and then rejoined the cast on stage. We arranged ourselves into a row and held one another's hands as if dolls cut from folded paper. Eliza waited for the applause to taper off, then tugged on the curtain ropes one last time. One of the pulleys tore loose from the ceiling, the rope coiled and snaked, and the curtain came down. Eliza, in full view of the audience then, waved. We bowed as a group, and the applause erupted anew. I let go of Clarice and Rosa's hands and motioned for Mr. Tinka to stand. He stood, turned to the audience, and, with a flair equal to the music he'd made, bowed deeply.

When the applause wound down, I stepped forward, almost tripping on a fold in the fallen curtain, and said, "We, the members of the Working Girls Social Club, thank you all for coming. And, thanks to the generosity of the Resting Room Advisory Council and the graciousness of our hostess, Eliza Moore, refreshments will be served in the main house directly." Ohs and ahs replaced the applause that had filled the air.

I looked to the back, where Mama was just rising from the velvet settee. I looked to the transom. If I could have split myself in two, half going one way, half the other, I would have.

Mama's eyes were watery, though, much to my relief, not

stricken. "That was beautiful, Hannah, the way they lit the candles."

I hugged Mama then, and she whispered, "Too bad your papa's so stubborn. He missed out on something special."

"I'm just glad you were here, Mama."

Megan and Joey ran up to us then. Joey's face and hands were smeared with icing. "I told him to use a fork, but he wouldn't listen," Megan said, her hands on her hips.

Mama began mopping Joey with her handkerchief.

"Whatever it is Joey took a bath in looks mighty good," Jake said.

Joey squirmed away from Mama. "They got teacakes. And lemonade, too."

Mama turned to me. "Would those be Flossy Zeller's secret recipe teacakes?"

"None other."

"Let's get on in there, then," Mama said. "But we mustn't dawdle. Your papa's likely itching to start for home."

"You all go on ahead. I'll join you shortly."

The print shop lights burned bright. Isaac's long face and the slump of his shoulders told me that Eliza had already shared the bad news.

Isaac came to stand close in front of me and held me with his eyes. "Guess I shouldn't have played that Hannah music last night."

"I needed to hear your music, Isaac, and you needed to play it. Sharing something that beautiful can never be wrong." I leaned forward and kissed his cheek then, right there in front of God and Eliza and Mrs. Richards.

I stayed with Isaac for as long as I dared, then, promising that I'd return once I'd seen my family off, I backed toward the door. The grin that had broken out on Isaac's face when I'd kissed him began to fade. Just before I turned to open the door, the corners of his mouth had sagged to forlorn, as did mine when I closed the door behind me.

Mama and the others were just coming into the resting room. "What's wrong, Hannah?" Mama said as she drew near. "You look like you've just lost your best friend."

How right she was, but I didn't tell her that, not then. My disappointment in Dru and my worry over what would come next for Isaac were still too raw and new.

Papa was standing beside the wagon. "Hannah, I'll be needing a private word with you." In the spare light of his lantern, I couldn't read his face, though his voice was stern.

I followed Papa down the drive, stopped when he stopped, braced myself against whatever he was about to say. He held the lantern so the light shone on my face. "I had a little business down at Shipmans, and Shipman asked if wasn't I a neighbor of Mr. Richards. I said I was, and he told me that Richards had been there earlier today and demanded to know where he could find a place called the Ladies Room. Said he'd heard that his wife was hiding out there. Is that true, Hannah? Is she here?"

My knees went weak. Too weak to hold up a lie. "Yes, Papa, she's here. Mr. Richards hurt her, and she needed a safe place to stay. Did Mr. Shipman tell Mr. Richards where to find the resting room?"

"Shipman steered him toward the public privy around back of the courthouse, but it's only a matter of time before someone sets him straight. Richards won't do you any harm, knows I'd string him up if he did, but if he does come around, you'd best stay out of his way."

"I'll be careful, Papa."

_____

When my family had gone on the their way, I hurried back to Isaac. My voice broke several times when I told him of Papa's awful news.

Isaac

THE NIGHT OF THE PLAY WAS THE LAST NIGHT I SPENT IN ELIZA'S house, but I didn't spend it sleeping.

Hannah didn't sleep, either. She spent that last night with me. After Ma and Eliza had gone up to bed, Hannah helped me roll my boat into the yard. I gave her a foot up, and then she lighted and set candles fore and aft. The sky showed a star here and there. We sat side by side, our arms touching.

I cleared my throat. "I've always known I'd leave here one day and take Ma with me. I just didn't know it would happen like this, happen so quick. Thought I'd have more time, thought we would have more time, and now I'm afraid I'll never see you again."

Hannah turned to me then and said, "We will see one another again, Isaac. We will be together again."

I didn't know what Hannah meant by that, but I sure wasn't going to let it drop. "Are you saying that maybe . . . someday?" Hannah smiled. The six-footed rabbit woke up and started in thumping hope against my ribs. I didn't try to tame it, just threw my arms around Hannah and pulled her against my chest. Her heart thumped back, and she pressed her cheek to mine. Her skin was as soft as the down on a baby chick. "I love you, Hannah Barnett," I whispered into her sweet-smelling hair.

I got a little worried that I'd spoken too soon when

Hannah didn't say she loved me, too. Then I felt why. Her shoulders shuddered and pretty soon her tears wetted my cheek. My Hannah was crying!

We sat that way for a good long while, then Hannah wiggled an arm free so she could reach for the hanky she always kept tucked up her sleeve. "Why not come with me now, today?" I asked.

"I'd love nothing more, Isaac, but I can't leave here just yet. I don't want clouds shading the rest of our lives. I want my papa's blessing."

The rabbit in my chest rolled over and died. "That'll be never, Hannah."

"My papa just needs more time. If I ran off with you now, I'd lose him. Lose Mama. If I wait, try to mend things, maybe I won't have to give up one kind of love for another."

"What if your pa doesn't come around, Hannah? What if he never gives us his blessing?"

Hannah answered my question with a kiss, and my lips answered hers back. And that kiss was the most beautiful thing on God's earth or in his heavens. The tallest mountain — the brightest shooting star!

I woke Ma just before dawn. When she rubbed her eyes open, she said she'd been dreaming she was riding on a train. That'd been the way I'd always dreamed we'd pull out of Prairie Hill, too. The conductor calling, "All aboard!" Folks waving from the platform. But that was before finding the boat. The boat that had kept me company every Sunday. The boat I'd told all my troubles to. I was leaving one of my girls behind; I wasn't about to leave them both.

By sunup, Mr. Tinka had helped me hitch her to the back of his wagon. Hannah was helping me load my gear, which was growing with every trip Eliza was making into and out of the house. She'd nearly emptied her pantry of foodstuffs and the Judge's closet of trousers and shirts. I had everything pretty well arranged — a canvas tent, which the Judge had used for fishing trips and which Eliza had also insisted I take, Ma's things, and my tools — when Eliza came running out, a paint pail swinging from one hand, a brush fisted in the other, and a bottle of something tucked under her arm. "It's bad luck to launch a boat until she's been christened."

"Paint large letters," Hannah said as I dipped the brush.

And that's what I did. I painted the letters big and bold and barn red. "How's that?" I asked Hannah when I was done.

Hannah's chin quivered, but she managed to say, "That suits me just fine."

Eliza handed me the bottle. "I don't have any champagne, but this bottle of Doctor Marvel's Miracle Medicinal Elixir might do in a pinch. I'm guessing it contains nearly as much alcohol."

I passed the bottle on to Hannah. "I'd like you to do the honors."

Hannah nodded, then two-fisted the bottle's neck and swung back. "I christen thee *Hannah's Fair Wind*," she said before bashing the bottle against the ridge board. Elixir splattered every which way. But the drops on Hannah's cheeks weren't elixir.

Hannah set all the ladies off crying, Ma and Eliza, Rosa and Mrs. Tinka. And one boy. If it hadn't been for Mr. Tinka stepping in and saying we needed to get on the road, we'd probably still be standing there, up to our ankles in eye water.

We must have made a sorry sight when we did finally pull away — the Tinka wagon in the lead, *Hannah's Fair Wind* trailing along behind. Ma sat tall and proud, shading herself under the fancy parasol Eliza had given her for a going-away gift. I sat at Ma's side, looking back, my eyes anchored to Hannah's and hers to mine until the distance broke us apart.

I took up my harmonica then and played Hannah music without stop until reaching the banks of the Big Blue River. I bid the Tinkas farewell, launched *Hannah's Fair Wind*, and then dropped the oars into the muddy water. The Big Blue, the Missouri, the Mississippi, and then Ma would be safe and I'd begin my wait.

PART IV

Fall 1888

Isaac

To Hannah Barnett By Telegraph,
from St. Joseph, Missouri

Prairie Hill, Nebraska September 10 1888 Rec'd
11:10 AM

Arrived St. Joe. Hole in hull. Laying over to
repair. Both well now. Letter to follow. Hope
all well with you. Isaac

***

To Hannah Barnett By Telegraph,
from Memphis, Tennessee

Prairie Hill, Nebraska September 28 1888 Rec'd
2:30 PM

Arrived Memphis. Promised letter jumped ship.
Doing odd jobs to buy dry supplies. Praying all
well with you. Isaac

***

To Hannah Barnett By Telegraph,
from New Orleans, Louisiana

Prairie Hill, Nebraska November 18, 1888 Rec'd
12:15 PM

New Orleans. Finally. Warm here. Lively music
all around. Letter when settled. Crazy from not
knowing how you are. Isaac

***

November 23, 1888

My Dearest Hannah,

I'll start this by saying that there hasn't been a day, an hour, or a minute since I left that I haven't thought of you. I was ready to turn around, hightail it back to you at least a hundred times, and I would have if it weren't for my ma. Ma hasn't been this happy since before Pa died. She says I should tell you that her face hurts from smiling so much.

The other thing you need to know right off is that this isn't the first letter I wrote. The first one is probably being read by a school of fish in the Gulf of Mexico about now. Had a little problem near St. Louis. Also had a little problem near Baton Rouge. Campfire got out of control, but I don't want to waste paper writing about all that.

And please, Hannah, don't let the sun set without writing me back. I'm going mad from needing to know that you are okay. Did Mr. Richards come around? If he made any threats against you or Eliza, then you've got to tell it to me straight, and I'll be on the next train headed north. What about the sheriff? Did he arrest Eliza for hiding me? Dru's ma, did she make good on her threat to close down the resting room? Dru, what's happened to her? And your pa, Hannah. Are things still going in the right direction with him? The working girls? Harmony School? That red-headed clod, Rusty Farley? I've got to know everything. Otherwise I'll imagine the worst like I've been doing ever since I left.

Here's the good news. I found work yesterday, as a boat builder's apprentice. Mr. Gluck, the owner of the boat works, took one look at *Hannah's Fair Wind*, patched hull and all, and hired me on the spot. I'll be making good pay, Hannah. When you're ready to tell your pa about me, make sure you tell him that, too.

Have also found a nice place for me and Ma to live — two furnished rooms above a bakery shop. Smells almost as good as when Mrs. Tinka was baking her bread in Eliza's kitchen. And there are big, sunny windows that aren't covered over with paper!

The weather is fine here. It's as warm today as Nebraska in May, and folks I've talked to say it hardly ever snows. Imagine that, Hannah. No more blizzards!

Everything's lush here. Moss-covered trees everywhere. Water everywhere, though a fellow told me to steer clear of the swamps — because of the alligators! Sure wouldn't mind getting a peek at one of those chompers. I've been to the Gulf of Mexico, Hannah, waded in waist-deep, just like you told me I should. You'd like the ocean, Hannah. It reminds me of the prairie, the way it goes on and on. Like the prairie, but without the plows.

Some of the folks here speak French and some speak

English and some speak what sounds like a mixing of the two. And oh the music, Hannah. Jazz. Started hearing it when me and Ma was still coming down the river, drifting out of hallows along the banks and in the wake of grandly lit riverboats that were churning upstream. It's music that reaches right inside you and touches your soul.

I miss you so much it hurts. Ma says that I need to be patient, that being apart will make our hearts grow even fonder. If my heart loved you any more than it already does, it would explode.

Forever yours,
Isaac

Hannah

December 8, 1888

My Dearest Isaac,

Your wonderful letter arrived a short while ago, and I have wasted only the minutes it took to read through it a dozen times before beginning this letter back to you.

New Orleans — the sights and sounds! I've always dreamed of such a place and now you are living there. I'm so glad for you and so relieved to know that you and your mother are safely settled. The telegrams you sent are worn thin and crumpled now, from carrying them in my pockets day after day. Without them I would surely have worried my apron hem to shreds. There is some fraying, I must admit, from imagining the trials of your journey.

I am missing you, terribly, but otherwise I am fine, truly I am. I fill my days with work. Nighttime is another story. Sometimes I'll forget, rush into the print shop expecting to find you there, or I'll hear a muffled sound in the night and think it is you stirring in your sleep. These are the most difficult moments. Nights are also my most cherished times because I now sleep with your pillow tucked under my head, and this had made for some lovely dreams.

Eliza has just come into the print shop (that is where I

am writing this letter), and she has told me to tell you that she sends her best.

Being the clever fellow that you are, you have guessed from this that Eliza is not in jail. Sheriff Tulley did come looking for you, not two hours after you left. Not finding you on the property, and having no evidence, other than hearsay, that Eliza had harbored a thief, the sheriff, winking, told Eliza that he supposed he wouldn't need to march her off to the jail. Mrs. Callahan's threat to close down the resting room was not successful, either. She tried, but the city attorney found no law forbidding a private property owner from inviting guests into her home. Eliza was required to obtain a permit for the market because money is exchanged for goods. This, too, went smoothly. The city attorney's wife is one of our best customers! A few members of the Betterment Society did stay away from the market in the first weeks, though most have since returned. There has been some whining, though, due to the absence of Mrs. Tinka's breads.

There was one threat Mrs. Callahan did manage to carry out. Dru is in Boston. I've received several letters from her. As always, she is making the best of her situation. She has befriended the young man who is the groundskeeper at the school and volunteers her free time teaching English to immigrant women at a settlement house. She plans to return to Prairie Hill for the Christmas holidays and has promised to stop by for a visit, "no matter what it takes." Any disappointment I might have felt the night of the play has long since faded, and I am so looking forward to seeing her again. Losing my best friend and my best (and only) beau at the same time was doubly heartbreaking.

My family is well. Harmony School has been rebuilt, a new teacher has been hired, so the younger children are back at their studies. Mama comes to town with the Zellers as often as she can, and we've had some wonderful visits.

Which brings me to my papa. The Sunday after you left, just as he was finishing his meal, I asked if I might have a private word with him. He nodded, then left the table and headed for the barn. I followed. Once there, I steadied myself, then told Papa all about you, Isaac. I told him about how you spent the summer at Eliza's and that you chose to hide rather than leave without your mother. I told him that you are not a thief, that the tools had belonged to your real father and not Mr. Richards. I told him that you are not at all like Mr. Richards and his boys, that you possess a fine character and a loving heart. I told him what a hard worker you are and about how you taught yourself boat-building by reading a book. I told him again that you had not shamed me the night of the blizzard, only kept me warm and alive. I told Papa that I was sorry I had deceived him with half-truths, sorry that I had disappointed him, and that I would try my best to again earn his trust. I finished by saying words I'd never said out loud to Papa before. I told Papa that I loved him. Papa listened, though he said nothing back, only turned and walked away. I expected just that. But I know he listened and that is a start.

I've told Mama all this and one thing I stopped short of telling Papa. I told her that, one day, you and I plan to meet again, and never to part. Mama cried. Sad tears, at first, then a small smile formed on her face and she said, "I'll be expecting you to bring my grandbabies for regular visits." I blushed.

And I am not the only Barnett girl blushing these days. Back in September, Rusty Farley asked Papa if he might call on Hester. Papa gave Rusty his blessing, and they do make a handsome couple.

Now, before I close, I must tell you of my morning. When I awoke, the first snow of the season was falling past my window. Wet, heavy flakes, much like the snow that fell on the morning of the blizzard. I closed my eyes, hoping it was only a dreadful dream, but when I opened them again, the snow was still coming down. I've planned for this day, Isaac, mentally practiced it as if a part in a play. I couldn't be sure if practice alone could turn my fear around. There was but one way to know for sure.

My footprints mapped a path as I moved away from the shelter of the buildings and into the open space of the lawn. I stopped and looked back. My path had not been erased. I walked on — until I had come to the place where town and prairie meet. I closed my eyes, lifted and turned my face to the north sky and then waited for Wild Wind's rasp and roar. I felt only the brush and heard only the whisper of Fair Wind's breeze. I imagined your hand in mine and together we crossed from lawn to prairie. On we walked, glancing back now and again and stopping only when the house had disappeared to white. You played Hannah music then, and I began to dance, round and round, tracing spirals in the snow. Round and round, until dizzy with the joy of it. We stayed there on the prairie for nearly an hour, and I could have stayed longer, would have, if not for you, Isaac. You whispered that there was a surprise waiting for me back at the house. And what a wonderful surprise your letter has been!

You need not worry, Isaac. I am still mindful of the dangers and promise to be careful. I know that Wild Wind is out there, somewhere. When she does blow in, I will not cower, nor will I be ladylike. I will dig in my heels, work the saliva around in my mouth — and spit in her face. Once for Jon and once for Jacob. I will turn every one of Eliza's gaslights to full wick and set a lighted candle at every window, then sit before the fire and muster every last ounce of my imagination to grow the light into a powerful beacon, send it shining and sailing out across the prairie. And beyond — send it all the way to New Orleans to light the eyes of the man I love — today, tomorrow, and forever!

Write often and at length, and I will do the same — until we are together again.

With all my love,
Hannah

The End

Author's Note

Though Hannah, Isaac, and all the characters in this novel are fictional, the blizzard that so profoundly affected their lives was a real event in history. On January 12, 1888, a fierce winter storm swept out of Canada and engulfed the states of the central plains — from the Rocky Mountains east to the Mississippi River; from the Canadian border south to Texas. Newspaper accounts from that time estimated the loss of life from five hundred to a thousand. Tragically, many of those who perished were school children, prompting some to name the storm "The School Children's Blizzard."

Today, if we want to know the weather forecast, we simply turn on the radio or television or visit a weather Web site on the Internet. Such was not the case in 1888. The look and color of the sky, the mercury rising or falling from the bulb of a thermometer, a sudden shift in speed or direction of the wind were the only forecasting tools available to individuals living on the plains.

Snow had fallen during the night of January 11–12, and it continued to fall, heavily at times, throughout the morning. Temperatures were unseasonably warm, ranging from the upper twenties to lower thirties across the region. The wind was southerly and light. With no hint of what was to come, farm children set off for school, some on horseback though most on foot, their lunch pails swinging at their sides. The distance to school varied from a few hundred feet to several miles. The majority of rural schoolhouses were one-room frame structures and were heated by wood or coal-burning stoves. At best, these stoves provided only modest heat in these often drafty buildings.

The storm moved from northwest to southeast at a rate of fifty miles per hour. Depending on the geographic location of a particular school, the storm struck at different times of day — morning in the central portions of the Dakotas, Nebraska, and Kansas; afternoon in the eastern sections of these same states.

Descriptions of the storm's arrival, however, were strikingly similar. A wall of heavy black clouds appeared on the northwest horizon. The wind shifted abruptly to the north and slammed into the schoolhouses with near-hurricane force. Walls shook and windows rattled as if struck by the open palm of a giant's hand. Many likened the wind's roar to that of a fast-moving freight train. Snow that earlier had lain harmlessly on the ground lifted and filled the air, reducing visibility to little more than an arm's length. Temperatures plummeted by as much as thirty degrees within minutes of the storm's arrival and continued to fall throughout the day and following night, reaching -30 in many regions by the morning of Friday, January 13.

Those caught out of doors when the blizzard struck

later gave chilling descriptions of their ordeal. The wind-driven snow so choked the air that the simple act of breathing was difficult. Eyelids froze shut. The hems of girls' long skirts crusted with snow and tangled about their ankles, pulling them down. Deep drifts created hidden, sinking traps. Feet and hands grew numb from the cold.

Survival, in large part, depended on the decisions individual teachers made that day. Keeping the children inside the schoolhouse until help arrived was the choice made by many. This was especially true for those schools that had an adequate supply of fuel on hand to keep the stove burning through the night. In many instances, fathers set out to fetch their children home by horse and sleigh. Some fought their way to the school, though others were forced to turn back when their horses refused to face into the ferocious wind or because the fathers themselves became lost.

There were teachers who, for various reasons, led their students into the storm. Minnie May Freeman, teaching at a school near Ord, Nebraska, was left with no choice when the wind ripped away a portion of the school's roof. Miss Freeman, still in her teens, led her sixteen pupils to a home a half-mile away. Many of the children suffered frostbite, but they were otherwise unharmed. Another story had a very different ending. Lois May Royce was teaching at a school near Plainview, Nebraska. When the storm hit, there were only three children at the school: Peter Poggensee, nine; Otto Rosberg, nine; and Hattie Rosberg, six. Having run out of wood for the stove, Miss Royce decided to lead the children to a farm that was only two hundred yards (two football fields) to the north. Blinded by the swirling snow, they wandered off course and became hopelessly lost, finally sinking into the snow near a haystack. By morning all three children had died. Miss Royce survived, but her feet were so badly frozen they required amputation.

Some teachers, perhaps not realizing the severity of the storm, promptly dismissed school and sent all the children home. Alone or in small family groups, many found their way by following fence lines or the stubbled rows of harvested corn stalks. Others, lost and weakened from hours of trudging through waist-deep drifts, survived through the night by burrowing into hay or straw stacks. Sadly, still others found no shelter of any kind. The Westphalen sisters, ages thirteen and seven, concerned about their widowed mother, convinced the teacher of their school near Rogers, Nebraska, to allow them to go out into the storm. When their bodies were discovered many days later, the younger girl was found wrapped in the older sister's coat.

No one living on the plains at that time was spared from the horror of the storm, be they in safe shelter or not. And no one forgot. In 1914, the last words of O. W. Coursey's dying mother were these — "Son, you will never know the burden that was lifted from my heart the next morning after the Big Blizzard, when I looked out and saw you four older children scampering home over the snowdrifts when I was positively sure you had all perished in the storm."

On January 12, 1940, fifty-two years after the storm, a group of Nebraskan survivors formed the "January 12, 1888, Nebraska Blizzard Club." Over the next several years, the club gathered personal recollections from hundreds of survivors and compiled their stories into a book titled *In All Its Fury: The Great Blizzard of 1888*. Their vision for the book was this: "The January 12, 1888, Blizzard Club wishes to preserve the records of the past because they will help us better to understand the present and the future. Yesterday has lessons for all of us, but tomorrow throws not one ray of light upon the problems of today."

In All Its Fury was reprinted in 1988 by J & L Lee Books, Lincoln, Nebraska. I found it to be an invaluable resource and recommend it to those who wish to learn more about this tragic storm.

On March 11–14, 1888, another horrific blizzard, the "Great White Hurricane," as it was called, paralyzed the East Coast of the United States, from the Chesapeake Bay to Maine. More than four hundred lives were reported lost.

As my character Hannah might say, "Wild Wind had a wickedly busy year."